Henry Allen Tupper

The Carpenter's Son

Henry Allen Tupper

The Carpenter's Son

ISBN/EAN: 9783337375454

Printed in Europe, USA, Canada, Australia, Japan

Cover: Foto ©Andreas Hilbeck / pixelio.de

More available books at **www.hansebooks.com**

THE CARPENTER'S SON.

Οὐκ οὗτός ἐστιν ὁ τοῦ τέκτονος υἱός;—Matt. xiii. 55.

BY

H. A. TUPPER.

———

BALTIMORE:
R. H. WOODWARD AND COMPANY.
1889.

INSCRIPTION.

I INSCRIBE THIS BOOK TO

𝔐𝔶 𝔅𝔢𝔩𝔬𝔳𝔢𝔡 𝔚𝔦𝔣𝔢,

WHO, AS THE MOST CONSTANT AND CONSCIENTIOUS

READER OF THE BIBLE THAT I HAVE

EVER KNOWN, IS AN

INSPIRATION TO THE STUDY OF THE SCRIPTURES,

WHOSE MAIN DOCTRINES AND FACTS,

WITH

SOME OF THE PRINCIPLES OF NATURE AND PROVIDENCE

RELATED TO THEM,

I HAVE TRIED TO GENERALIZE IN THIS VOLUME,

TO THE

HONOR OF HIM WHOSE NAME IT BEARS.

THE AUTHOR.

RICHMOND, VA., Aug. 28th, 1888.

CONTENTS.

CHAPTER XII.

CHAPTER XIII.

CHAPTER XIV.

CHAPTER XV.

CHAPTER XVI.

CHAPTER XVII.

CHAPTER XVIII.

CHAPTER XIX.

CHAPTER XX.

CHAPTER XXI.

CHAPTER XXII.

CHAPTER XXIII.

CHAPTER XXIV.

THE CARPENTER'S SON.

CHAPTER I.

STRANGE AND SUGGESTIVE STORY.

Is not this the carpenter ?—Mark vi. 3.

IN the Apocryphal New Testament this story is told: The king of Jerusalem ordered Joseph of Nazareth to build for him a throne to fit a certain place in the palace where the king was accustomed to sit. After two years Joseph finished the throne, but found to his dismay that it did not fit the place, as the king had ordered, by two spans. Joseph's son bade his father to take hold on one side of the throne while he took hold on the other, and stretched it until it made a perfect fit. The story continues in these quaint words : " The throne was made of the same wood which was in being in Solomon's time, namely, wood adorned with various shapes and figures."

This is a strange story, and none the less so because material used by the royal builder of the first temple is associated with Joseph's son, who is called in the gospel according to Mark "the carpenter," ($\delta \ \tau \acute{\epsilon} \varkappa \tau \omega \nu$) and who

appeared in public first in the temple, saying, "Wist ye
not that I must be about my Father's business?" and
whose zeal for the temple was so great that beholders
were reminded of the Messianic prediction, "The zeal
of thine house hath eaten me up."

A suggestive feature of the legend is that the skill of
the son was greater than that of the father. This is
not strange. The trade of Joseph's son was given him
not merely by his reputed father, but by his real Father
—as much as was divinely given the vocation of Beza-
leel and Aholiab, builders of the tabernacle, "in whom
the Lord put wisdom and understanding to know how
to work all manner of work for the service of the
sanctuary;" and the business of Hiram, who, "filled
with wisdom and understanding," wrought the skilled
and divinely-ordered work of the temple of Solomon.

And need not this to have been just so? That eternal purpose which planned the whole creation and
history of the universe from eternity to eternity, and
the unfailing providence, which superintends the execution of that plan from the birth and work and death of
the least animalcule to the origin and movement and
destiny of worlds and systems of worlds, must have
determined and superintended all that pertained to the
incarnation of the Son of God, and, among other things,
the occupation of his boyhood and earlier manhood
to which he was adapted no doubt by special mental
and physical abilities. He that wings the butterfly and
shapes the leaf for certain ends, had positive reason
why Jesus of Nazareth should be a carpenter and a

carpenter's son, and more skilled and powerful, as the legend has it, than his carpenter father.

And what was that reason? There is a doctrine of correspondence between the material and the immaterial, between the natural and the spiritual, which, though it may be pressed too far, has in it a basis of truth. The material and the natural are the phenomena of the immaterial and the spiritual, and are sometimes their representatives and symbols. It is designed by the universal author that we should pass from the obvious to the recondite, from the manifest to the hidden, from the human to the divine. Hence the trade of this so-called "carpenter" of Nazareth was given to or assumed by him because it was the best practical representation of what he was really and essentially. He was a maker, a builder. Who built the spire of grass with its measured frame and its fibrous covering and its graceful proportions and its complete symmetry; and the more elaborately constructed tree with its root-foundation, its supporting trunk, its bracing branches and twigs and its foliage-covered whole; and the boundless forests of nature and the plantations of man—these buildings that make up the vegetable kingdom of human science? Who built the pebble with its component parts, the rock with its perfectly adjusted atoms, the mountain with its well laid strata, and the stupendous construction of the waters of the deep? And who fabricated the marvellous structures and organisms of bird and beast and fish and man? Is there any human edifice so accurate in proportions, so harmonious in adjustment, so adapted in its uses, so perfect in its completeness as these constructions? And are not these as psalms and hymns in Nature's Temple? He that built the spire of grass built our globe, and built all worlds; and did he not put them together into a grand Temple for the divine glory? In the Old Testament he is called Wisdom, and he says of himself, "I was set up from everlasting, from the beginning, or ever the earth was. . . . And by wisdom the Lord founded the earth and established the heavens." In the New Testament he is called the Word, of whom it is written, "In the beginning was the word, and the word was with God, and the word was God. . . . All things were made by him, and without him was not anything made that was made." And as to the temple-idea, why did he make anything—everything? In pondering aright this question we must conclude, sooner or later, that he made all things for the praise of his own name; which accords with the divine declaration, "for of him and through him and to him are all things, to whom be glory forever. Amen." Hence we read that the whole world is full of his glory. And is not "the world full of his glory" the best possible description of a grand and universal temple?

And when disaster came upon this temple of nature by a vital part falling into ruin, the same builder came again to rebuild, saving a part of the fallen material; to construct a temple vaster and more enduring— a temple whose corner-stone and foundations and materials and completion are described in the gospel, and the architect and builder of which is plainly declared to be this Carpenter's Son, called in contempt ὁ τέκτων, as he was called "the sinner's friend," and yet called so truly, though he might have been called more truly (ὁ ἀρχιτέκτων) "the Master Builder."

The story suggests also that the Carpenter's Son did work other than house-building. And this is the import of the term by which he is called. He is not called by the term (ὁ οἰκοδομός) house-builder, but by the broader term rendered in the gospel "the carpenter," ὁ τέκτων, which derived from τεύχω, to make, to construct, to build, means the maker, the constructor, the builder. This symbolizes more perfectly the varied and vast workmanship of the eternal Son in his creative and recreative office. He makes thrones and nations, and plans and systems, and races angelic and redeemed—the last race, a special one that makes applicable to him the classic phrase ὁ τέκτων γένους; as well as, as has been said, worlds combined and reconstructed, comprehending these things and all things harmonious and praise-giving into a temple universal and everlasting, of which he is, as I have said, really ὁ ἀρχιτέκτων, rendered in the New Testament "the master-builder." As may be convenient, I shall use the terms ὁ τέκτων and even ὁ ἀρχιτέκτων as interchangeable with "the carpenter" or "the carpenter's son."

And the fitness of the correspondence between the trade of the Carpenter's Son and the ordained work of the Son of the Divine Creator and Preserver of all, is seen more clearly as we reflect how carpentry implies in its results, creation and construction, and harmonization and unity, and perpetuation by the application of intelligence and skill and wisdom; the very results of the eternal maker-ship, whose accomplishment is by the wisdom and power and all the attributes of the Divine Mind. This symbol also meets the primal law of divine symbols, viz., that the symbol and the symbolized must be in different kingdoms. No symbol of the essential Divine Maker could be more complete than "the carpenter's son."

As to the main point of the legend, that the throne of the father was by the son stretched out and made to meet exactly the royal order, has it not an ample realiza-tion in the application to this "son of David" of the divine prophecy, " For unto us a child is born, unto us a son is given, and the government shall be upon his shoulder. . . . Of the increase of his government and peace there shall be no end, upon the throne of David, and upon his kingdom to order it and to establish it, with judgment and with justice, from henceforth even forever " ?

CHAPTER II.

CONSTRUCTIVE PRINCIPLE UNIVERSAL.

*For every house is builded by some man; but he that built all things is
God.*—Heb. iii. 4.

LEAVING the apocryphal story, let us glance at the
constructive principle which pervades the divine
works themselves, and makes them to be not only fit
instruments but striking symbols of the Carpenter's Son
—the grand living and symbolic representative of the
essential constructiveness of the divine nature.

The animal germ, so small that a million of them
may rest on the point of a needle, no sooner comes into
existence than it begins to build, with marvellous skill,
a home for itself—though it may be in the tissues and
vesicles of human nerves. The polyp unites with its
fellow polypi and builds coral reefs on which navies are
wrecked and kingdoms are founded. The ant is a
famous builder. Solomon says: "The conies are a
feeble folk, but they build their houses in the rocks."
In his fourth Georgic, Virgil declares the office of the
home-bee,

> "To fortify the comb, to build the wall,
> To prop the ruins lest the fabric fall."

The constructions of the bird of the air and the beast
of the field are celebrated in holy writ.

7

The acorn and the sap build the oak; the zephyr and the sunbeam construct the tempest. And when we see the constructive power of light, and sound, and electricity, and magnetism, and the elements that make up earth, and water and atmosphere, we begin to think that this constructiveness is the primal law of the forces of nature.

Man is a constructive being so far as he is in his normal state. Abnormally he is a destroyer, which is his unnaturalness. He is a material builder. He builds houses, and bridges, and roads, and factories, and constitutions and governments, and posterity—the Greek phrase, $\tau \acute{\epsilon} \varkappa \tau \omega \nu \ \gamma \acute{\epsilon} \nu o \upsilon \varsigma$, is originally applied to him. He himself is physically built. Landon says: "The generality of Genoese country-women are strongly built"—assuming a Genoese country-woman to be a man! Man is a metaphorical, mental, moral, ideal builder. He builds fortune and fame, arguments and hopes, character and destiny, for weal or woe, according as he builds on the sand or on the rock. So inveterate a builder is he, that when he cannot build anywhere else, *he builds castles in the air!*

Man's art is but the imitation of the building of nature, and his science is only certain constructions of the principles on which are erected the edifices of creation.

So dominant is this building passion, in the mould of which his ideas and conduct and character are cast, that no sooner was Cain driven from "the presence of the Lord" than he built a city; and the first device of man after the flood was to build a tower which should defy another such catastrophe on earth. Defeated by the confusion of tongues, he began to construct separate languages and nationalities. And in what does the glory of human history consist if not in the monuments, the palaces, the temples, the pyramids, the cities, the institutions, the systematized learning, exhumed from the earth or flourishing upon it? And worthy of note is it, that the oldest and most general human organization has for its symbols the implements of the builder's craft, and is known by the name of Free-masons, who, by the way, claim Solomon the royal builder of the first temple, and the greatest symbol of "the Carpenter's Son," as their "First Most Excellent Grand Master."

Angels are inspired by the same constructive power, and when they become demons they employ this faculty to construct destruction, as Milton sings:

"Nor aught avail'd him now
To have built in heaven high towers, nor did he 'scape
By all his engines, but was headlong sent,
With his industrious crew, to build in hell."

And whence this universal building principle? God is the great essential and eternal *builder* of the universe. I emphasize builder. Some one calls the worlds God's thoughts. The truth is more exactly expressed thus, "Every house is builded by some man, but he that built all things is God." God does not only create, he builds. He did not call into existence the whole world, he built it. He built it upon the same principles of mathematics and mechanics that the throne, the palace, the temple is built on. Some say that it was built in six days; others, in 200,000,000 years; but all agree that the world was built !

Hence the most perfect representation of the divine nature was "the carpenter's son," whose life and whose death were instruments of the vastest and most glorious upbuilding ; and the sum of whose doctrine—on this line—was, that the evil principle antipodal to God's constructive nature, which had entered the world, would be eternally expressed by destroying fire; and that this essential constructiveness of the divine nature would be expressed, as I have said and re-said, by this Temple, heavenly and eternal, of which he is "the master builder."

I spoke of the germ and acorn, and bird and beast, and man and angel being builders.   But their constructiveness is only the impress of the divine constructiveness wrought into the constitution of his creatures, that they might reflect this essential attribute of their Creator, and have stamped upon their face, as the mission of their existence, the service and symbolization of the great symbol of the divine energy, "the carpenter's son," by whom all these ten thousand times ten thousand workers, God-ordained and God-marked as his servants, are actually and incessantly employed for the erection of the referred-to Temple, universal and eternal, the model of which, let me say with reverence, is the Divine being himself, in whom all live and move, and have their being. Hence God's image, man, was fearfully and wonderfully made, not merely as a kind of creator, maker, builder, ruler, but also a sort of microcosmic Temple of whose restored nature it is written, "Ye also as lively stones are built up, a spiritual house . . . . builded together for an habitation of God through the Spirit." And hence, the Son of man said to his enemies, referring to his human life, "Destroy this Temple and in three days I will raise it up." The Jews thought he referred to their Temple which had been "forty and six years in building," but they knew not of that temple of which Paul said, "Know ye not that ye are the temple of God, and that the Spirit of God dwelleth in you? If any man defile the temple of God, him shall God destroy; for the temple of God is holy, which temple ye are,"— a temple which was a living miniature of that Temple eternal and divine, of which Solomon's temple was a material symbol.

CHAPTER III.

PREVAILING SUFFERING AND DEATH.

The whole creation groaneth and travaileth in pain together until now.—Rom. viii. 22.

THE office of the Carpenter's Son was not only to do, but to endure and to die. Suffering was not a part of his essential self as was his constructiveness. But, it was a part of his vicarious experience and accomplishment, as necessary as his work of edification. It was the corner-stone of the great edification. And, because of its awful mysteriousness, as well as its unsurpassed momentousness, it has as profound reason to be represented in the very frame-work of nature as the constructiveness of the divine nature. And does it not seem, apart from Bible-doctrine, almost, if not quite, as far-reaching? There is no created life in this world without suffering and death. Life itself is scientifically defined as a combination of faculties for the resistance of death. Looking beyond our narrow world, we see this evil everywhere abounding. The economy of creation and construction, as well as of universal restitution, seems inwrought with this terrible experience. So far as can be read from nature, destruction appears co-extensive with creation. Where is the creature, animate or inanimate, not subject to death?

12

Did not death come before the human race, as geology
and demonology attest? Has it not invaded the shining
ranks around the eternal throne?   And how much has
suffering and death to do with the origin and history
and destiny of the new race on earth?   How much has
death to do with all life—natural, spiritual, everlasting?
Is not the renewed world to be born out of universal
death? It is not strange that the human intellect, unen-
lightened from above, has thought that evil is eternal ;
that life sprang out of death, as light comes out of
darkness, and should ask, Can God suffer?   To the
natural mind there can be no more fathomless mystery
than this inherent experience and state of things terrestrial and super-terrestrial.   The face of nature, animate
and inanimate, is stamped with sadness and woe.   From
a human stand-point, the mystery is intensified by the
fact that the only holy being that ever trod our earth,
was himself "a man of sorrow, and acquainted with
grief."   Vain is it that Dr. Henry M. Field, in the
North American Review, August, 1887, urges against
Col. Robert G. Ingersoll, his striking and beautiful
argument from the character and teachings of the Carpenter's Son.   Read it :

"All who have made a study of the character and
teachings of Christ, even those who utterly deny the
supernatural, stand in awe and wonder before the
gigantic figure which is here revealed.   Renan closes
his 'Life of Jesus' with this as the result of his long
study : 'Jesus will never be surpassed.   His worship
will be renewed without ceasing ; His story (légende)

will draw tears from beautiful eyes without end ; His sufferings will touch the finest natures ; *all the ages will proclaim that among the sons of men there has not risen a greater than Jesus ;'* while Rousseau closes his immortal eulogy by saying, '*Socrates died like a philosopher, but Jesus Christ like a God!*'

"Here is an argument for Christianity to which I pray you to address yourself. As you do not believe in miracles, and are ready to explain everything by natural causes, I beg you to tell us how came it to pass that a Hebrew peasant, born among the hills of Galilee, had a wisdom above that of Socrates or Plato, of Confucius or Buddha? This is the greatest of miracles, that such a being has lived and died on the earth."

Cogent and striking as is the argument, the death to which it refers, falling in with the universality of suffering and death, rebuts it, in the mind of skepticism, as inconsistent with the point the argument would establish. Is this suffering and death so universal that even the wisest and best, compared to "a God," cannot escape its omnipresent and omnipotent grasp? Does it compass the Creator of the Universe? Can the God of true religion suffer and die? Is sorrow and death more wide-spread than moral evil, said to be its source? If they are everlasting, as admitted, why not also eternal? And in view of the shedding of blood being a foundation principle of universal religion, and a positive command of the Almighty himself, Col. Ingersoll actually perpetrates the hideous sneer: "What do you think of Abraham, Jephthah, Jehovah?" The good use of this bad question, which Mr. Gladstone well rebukes and turns bravely against the adversary, (*North American Review*, July 1888,) is, to give the greatest emphasis to the fact—the most terrible fact of this suffering and death, which sweeps over the trinity of worlds, earth, and heaven and hell!

But, deep and dark as this mystery is, it is as explicable as the universality of the constructive element of nature. It is not perfectly explained by the existence of moral evil, though without moral evil there might have been no pain and death. It cannot be thus explained, because suffering and death may be the expression of the noblest virtues, may consist with the profoundest satisfaction, and be the companion of absolute and perfect holiness. But, may it not be expounded by the fact that the atonement wrought by the Carpenter's Son, involving the costliest blood and exceeding sorrow, was wrapped up with the love-nature of this eternal being as truly as his essential constructiveness, the Lamb being slain before the foundation of the world? And widespread nature, stamped with the divine constructiveness, is also stamped with this eternal idea and purpose and plan and fact of sorrow and death, in order to prepare for, and to be sympathetic with, the world's greatest event, and to reflect the crowning glory of the great lover and sufferer of the universe. As for the human race, they must be, not only "workers together with him," but "sufferers with him," in order to be glorified with him. They are to know the fellowship of Christ's sufferings and death, as a part of their edification into the likeness of their Lord, whose passive virtues were most conspicuous as representative of the most glorifying patience and long-suffering of the divine nature. God is not only the world's maker: it is written "God is love." Thus the universe was designed to be symbolic, not only of the divine building-essence, represented in the Carpenter's Son, but of the eternally ordained Carpenter's Son crucified, whom Holman Hunt does not paint merely as the young artisan of Nazareth, but with outstretched arms throwing on the wall the figure of a cross! The dedication of Solomon's symbolic Temple was signalized by his sacrificing, as it is written, "sheep and oxen that could not be told or numbered for multitudes."

CHAPTER IV.

THE SYMBOL—SOLOMON.

A shadow of things to come.—Heb. x. 1.

IN the history of our race there have been two re-
nowned builders representing the Carpenter's Son—
Noah, the builder of that antediluvian ship, in which
a part of the material of human nature was saved
for reëdification; and the royal builder of the first
Temple, which was to symbolize the reconstructed and
more glorious Temple and kingdom whose throne, like
the throne in the legend, stretched out by Joseph's son,
was to be an enlargement of the throne of Solomon's
father; whose headstone was to be brought out with
shoutings, "Grace, grace upon it;" and whose foundations
were to be laid in the blood of its builder—strikingly
represented by the countless bloody offerings of Solomon's Temple, the key-note to whose essential and perpetual service of blood was given at its dedication, of
which it is written, "And Solomon offered a sacrifice of
peace-offerings which he offered unto the Lord, two and
twenty thousand oxen and a hundred and twenty thousand sheep. So the king and all the children of Israel
dedicated the house of the Lord."

That Solomon, as the builder of the Temple, was a
symbol of the great Architect of the universe, repre-

sented in the Carpenter of Nazareth there is cumulative evidence.

His names Jedidiah and Solomon, meaning the Beloved and Peace, how suggestive of the "Beloved of the Father," "the Prince of Peace!"

His extraordinary gift was wisdom—the very name by which the worlds were made—which gift was given him not as a part of himself, but, as the gift of tongues and prophecy were given to apostles and prophets, as something added to the real character for a specific purpose. Hence, while Solomon was the wisest of men, he committed abominable follies, just as apostles and prophets were never equal in themselves to the inspiration of their tongues and pens. Solomon's follies were allowed that it might appear that his wisdom was not personal but symbolic.

Solomon was born and succeeded to David's throne in order that he might build the Temple. His father said to him, "Take heed now, for the Lord hath chosen thee to build an house for the sanctuary; be strong and do it." Hence, almost all the preparations and directions of David for his succeeding son had reference to this building, which was the signalizing work of Solomon's reign.

The Temple itself was symbolic—"a figure for the time then present"—symbolic as to its departments and offices and ceremonies, symbolic in its silent construction, in its materials brought from afar, in the multitudes engaged in its erection, and most especially in its sacrifices of the lamb of atonement, for which it was mainly erected. Its divinely-given model suggested that it was a symbol ; but the divine declaration is that it was "a shadow of good things to come." And the Temple a symbol, why not its builder?

And was Solomon's shocking fall symbolic of the Carpenter's Son falling a victim to the powers of sin and hell, that hung him up as a malefactor between two thieves on the accursed tree as a lasting spectacle to heaven and earth?

I need not refer to the tender-aged Solomon's saying, when he ascended the throne, "I am but a child;" and the Carpenter's Son being a child indeed when he appeared first in the temple; and to Solomon's Temple lasting in its completeness the number of years that the Master-builder tabernacled in the flesh. But I must refer to the more significant, if not conclusive fact, that these momentous words of God referring to Solomon, are expressly applied in the epistle to the Hebrews to the Christ who is often called the son of David, "He shall be my son and I will be his father." The whole passage reads: "He shall build a house for my name, and he shall be my son and I will be his father, and I will establish his throne over Israel forever."

And was not Solomon's glory in this fact of his being the symbol of the great architect and builder of the world?

There was glory in his riches, which were greater than the riches of any living man; glory in his wisdom, for he was wiser than all the wise men of the east; glory in his reign of peace, his luxurious court, his splendid structures and cities, and his world-wide fame which attracted to him the kings of the earth; great was the glory of the house which he built unto the Lord, as the only spot on earth where there was a general localization of religious thoughts and sentiments with regard to the true God, and a visible manifestation of Jehovah, and whither representatives from all nations were to go to worship—a house which billions of money and the best architectural skill made more splendid than the Athenian Parthenon, the Ephesian Temple of Diana, the Olympian, or Roman Capitoline Temple of Jupiter— perhaps the most splendid edifice on the face of the earth! The glory of all this was great. But above all this glory of his person, his court, his works, his reign, and the Temple itself, was the glory that all these gifts and possessions were designed and used to make Solomon the most glorious symbol of the universal builder and architect!

This makes Solomon a central figure of the world's history. This connects him with the constructive principle of the universe in all its varied departments; of which principle he himself was the most distinguished human illustration as the architect and builder of the more perfect model of the kingdom of heaven. There were other symbols of the maker of the heavens and the earth—symbols of some quality of his nature, some doctrine of his truth, some event of his reign on earth. But this man symbolized the Maker himself in his most comprehensive attributes and plans and executions! Hence, if the glory that invested Solomon seems almost supernatural, it was not more glorious than was meet in view of his God-symbolizing office !

But why this consideration of the symbol Solomon? Attention is directed to the great symbol in order to elevate to the greater symbolized—to the symbolized Master-builder, who, prompted by that constructive and benevolent instinct of the divine nature represented in the countless works of his hand, whereby all things were created for the happiness of the creature and the glory of the Creator, undertook according to an eternal plan to realize by his own personal labors and sacrifices, with the coöperation of the other persons of the Godhead and the subordination of the divinely derived constructive principle of all creatures, a perfect and perpetual temple of worship and praise, in which should be gathered all that honor God, and which should resound with halle-lujahs to Him that sitteth upon the throne forever !

The use of this symbol is to induce the intelligent seeker after truth, as Solomon was, to study the autobi-ographies of the great Master-builder—nature, provi-dence and revelation—wherein all available truth is found ; and to consecrate all studies, whether physical or metaphysical, artistic or scientific, philological or philosophical, ethnological or theological, typical or anti-typical, to the energizing and directing of the inherent and ineradicable constructive principle of his nature—so industriously, so earnestly employed for mere present and perishing upbuilding—to this God-ordained up-building, personal, social, spiritual, ecclesiastical, national, universal, everlasting, divine ! Great was the glory of

Solomon; but of the least of the Master-builder's works —the lily of the field—he himself said, "Solomon in all his glory was not arrayed like one of these." Great was his wisdom; but, declared the Master, "Behold a greater than Solomon is here!"—even the builder and architect of that temple universal and everlasting, of whom Solomon, with his splendid greatness, was only a dim shadow, a perishing symbol.

CHAPTER V.

ON EARTH.

L ET us take a general view of this being as he walked among the children of men.

HIS FAMILY.

Who is my mother or my brethren?—Mark iii. 33.

In the first chapter of his biography we see a record of his family running through more than fifty generations—from Joseph to Abraham. Indeed, it runs back, as another biographer shows, to Adam himself. This makes his descent more than royal—it makes it intensely human. He is identified thus with the whole race of man. He is the living link of the human brotherhood universal. Nothing that concerns man can he be indifferent to. Hence, his whole life was devoted to the interests of his fellows—feeding, healing, teaching gratuitously, laboriously, and despite lack of appreciation and even gross injustice. He was the realization of the ideal when God said, "Let us make man in our own image." Many are the features of interest in his family-record, but the feature of greatest interest is that the culmination of the grand descent from patriarchs, prophets and royal names, should be in Joseph, the carpenter of Nazareth.

But the same chapter of his biography declares the

stranger things, that his mother was a virgin, and his father the Holy Ghost. Hence, while he was subject to Mary and Joseph for most of his earthly life, and in his death, made provision for his widowed mother, he did not hesitate to leave them in his childhood to attend to the business of his Father in heaven, and to exclaim with regard to true worshippers of God, "Behold my mother and my brethren!" The trend of his whole career on earth was illustrative of his own exposition of his terrestrial mission, "Lo, I come to do thy will, O God." What that will is, the world's history of progressive edification and the universe's prospective reconstruction, all by this divine son and universal Architect, is a sufficient reply.

But this does not exhaust his family relations. There is another family besides the human and divine, composed of the worshippers of God, whether on earth or in heaven, a spiritual family as opposed to the carnal family of fallen angels and unbelieving men, and he is of this family the acknowledged and worshipped head and founder.

Hence the hostility of such sin-desperadoes as Herod the Great—representing the destructive element of moral evil—who would slay him; the terror with which he filled demons, who knew his constructive and living power better than Herod did; and hence, his many spiritual and mysterious acts, and institutions, and doctrines, as for example, his baptism, the Lord's Supper, his forty days' fast and temptation, his revolutionary sermon on the mount, his preaching the advent of the

kingdom of heaven, his bloody sweat and agony of
Gethsemane, his crucifixion on Calvary with the mystic
words, "It is finished." Hence, the many prophecies
with regard to his advent, the coming of the Magi to
worship him, the adoration of the angels, the confession
representing all worshippers on earth, "My Lord and
my God," and his last, and grand commission to all ages
of reconstructed humanity, to make his name "great
unto the ends of the earth."

HIS NAME.

He called his name Jesus.—Matt. i. 25.

"What is in a name?" The grammarian may give
one answer, the historian another, and the philosopher
still another. But the divine view of names seems to
imply that the person himself is involved in his name
when divinely given. Hence the baptismal formula,
"Into the name of the Father, Son and Holy Spirit,"
means into the Divine Trinity. So the words of Luke,
"the number of names together were about one hundred
and twenty," Acts i. 15, which signifies that the number
of disciples present was about one hundred and twenty.
Are less significant, for instance, the names already
mentioned, Adam, Solomon, Jesus? The last name is
certainly synonymous with the named himself, who, as
his name denotes, is the Saviour of the fallen and
ruined race of man. This is confirmed by his other
name, Emmanuel, which is interpreted, "God with us."
And might not his many appellations, Wonderful,
Counsellor, Mighty God, Everlasting Father, Prince of

Peace, the Lord Jesus Christ, be paraphrased the Wonderful Planner and Almighty Maker and Generator—the Peaceful Ruler of a kingdom founded on the life and death of the anointed Son of man and Son of God? Nor are any of the elements of these comprehensive titles lacking in the descriptive and all comprehending title of ὁ τέκτων in the broad sense of the ἀρχιτέκτων of, not only the original universe, but of the new heavens and the new earth wherein dwelleth righteousness, to be realized in the dispensation of the fulness of times when all things in heaven and in earth shall be gathered together in him, their life being hid with Christ in God.

HIS EARLY LIFE.

And Jesus increased in stature and in wisdom, and in favor with God and man.—Luke ii. 52.

What must have been the early life of such a being? What the inner life of consciousness, of meditation, of purpose, of varied and unutterable experience; what the outer life of fidelity to duty, of holy service, of preparation for his great life-mission! We are prepared for the statements that he was "subject to his parents," and that he "increased in wisdom and stature, and in favor with God and man." Both tables of the law were perfectly kept, which was one of his instruments for the world's restoration. Nor would it have seemed strange if, in connection with his physical development affirmed, it had been stated that his carpentry had made him famous for its fidelity and perfection. These works of his hands, connected in consciousness with the analogous and more momentous works of his future mission, must have been invested with something of sacredness which should elevate manual toil among men, and which, perhaps, allies in heart this sacred mechanic with the heart of a world toiling for the necessities of life, and to which he would be a solace, model and inspiration. And may we not dare the imagination that, while he was driving the symbolic plane or saw, or wielding the equally symbolic hammer or mallet, he was in holy contemplation of the mammoth construction to be wrought by the cross of Calvary?

PICTURE OF HIM.

Is not this the carpenter's son?—Matt. xiii. 55.

Hunt's painting of the young mechanic stretching himself and throwing on the wall the shadow of a cross, to which reference has been made, has been adversely criticised, but it illustrates several points suggested by the early life of the Carpenter's Son.

It illustrates the duty of labor. It was a Jewish maxim, that the man who does not teach his son a trade teaches him to steal. God commands, "Six days shalt thou labor." Not only self-support, but labor for others is at the foundation of manly character. Without it and the sterling qualities implied, ornamentation of body or mind is as a wreath around a column veneered and hollow.

It illustrates the dignity of labor. The noblest minds—those who have been masters through the ages, by observing the divine law, " whosoever will be chief among you let him be your servant"—have been the most laborious of men. God is the great laborer whose workshop, as we have seen, is the universe. His record-book opens sublimely, "In the beginning God created the heaven and the earth."

The picture suggests, by the presence of the cross, how broad may be the application of the laws of the world to the science and art of the mechanic's vocation. Those tools on the carpenter's bench were handled by his intelligence and skill, in making, perchance, the plow and the yoke, in building, perchance, the bridge and the house, in accordance with principles of mathematics and mechanics known by the workman to be involved in the construction of the globe—the creation of the physical world, principles known also by him to be sometimes analogous to, and always in harmony with laws of the metaphysical world, in which that instrument shadowed on the wall was to work out a construction destined to plow up and subdue the ends of the earth, to bridge over a fathomless abyss, and to erect a house not made with hands eternal in the heavens. Though infidel, the people of Nazareth seemed to connect the mechanics and the miracles of Jesus as they ask, "Is not this the carpenter, the son of Mary? What wisdom is this which is given unto him that even such mighty works are wrought by his hands?" Note the expression, mighty works *wrought by his hands*. The artist was not so far astray when he associated on his canvas the carpenter and the cross.

But there was a characteristic of the Carpenter's Son misrepresented by this painting, if the mechanic's stretching himself was designed to suggest any relaxation of mind. His mind was never relaxed. It was intently and constantly fixed on the gigantic work he came to do. This explains many of his paradoxical and parabolical doctrines, and expounds his often strange and superhuman conduct, which confused his friends, made his family think that he was "beside himself," and gave occasion to his malicious adversaries to publish that he was possessed of the devil. He was the impersonation of faith which is "the substance of things hoped for, the evidence of things not seen."

HIS PUBLIC CAREER.

Who went about doing good.—Acts x. 38.

When the Carpenter appeared publicly in his mission, he announced it to be the establishment of a kingdom spiritual, universal and everlasting, upon his dual sonship with man and God, which gave efficacy to his own voluntary and substitutionary immolation.

His workman's garb proclaimed him a man of the people. He knew that human revolutions do not begin at the apex but at the base of society; that the man who accomplishes great enterprises must lay hold of the people. He had been called by Simeon "the glory of his people Israel," and he manifested abundantly his zeal for them, for example, by his cleansing the temple with a scourge of cords. But he was also called by this man of God, "a light to lighten the Gentiles."

Hence, his genealogy was traced—as has been seen—not only to David and Abraham but to Adam, and even to God. He was a Jew but he was more than a Jew—he was a man ; and a man fit to be the head of the human race. His associates were Peter and James and John, not because they were fishermen, and thus training to be fishers of men, but because they were men—not dignitaries whose manhood was in danger of being swallowed up by perfunctory observances, but men simple and outright, of whose infirmities he was touched with a feeling, and with whose temptations he was also tempted. He thus identified himself with the essence of humanity, which was laying a corner-stone in the foundation he came to lay. Hence, when he was born, angels shouted, "on earth peace, good will toward men;" and he delighted to call himself "the Son of man."

And never man spake and did as this man. His words were as plow-shares tearing up the old foundations of false philosophy and religion, with regard to man's duty and destiny, and teaching that his only hope was in reconciliation with God and restoration to his image, made possible by vicarious atonement and the regenerating and sanctifying influences of the Holy Spirit. His deeds amazed the people, but they were only prophetic of greater things, as cleansing man of the malady of sin, hushing the storming passions of the nations, and exorcising the god of this world by the bloody sweat of Gethsemane, and the awful tragedy of Calvary, which not only rocked the earth and blotted out the sun and shook the dead out of their graves, but rent the vail of the Temple from top to bottom, and thus declared that free access to God was now secured to the race of man. He established his sonship with God as well as with man, which gave all efficacy to his sacrifice, and "upon this rock" he said, "I will build my church, and the gates of hell shall not prevail against it."

But in the pursuit of his building mission, he made also selection of material on which he was to work. As might be supposed, this selection was from the lower ranks of life. Thus he taught that, according to the economy of grace, the most favored of this world are not adjudged as necessarily the most favored of the world to come. He taught thus also, that the humblest and lowest need not despair, but may come in hope to the Father above and be wrought into the great fabric of his praise. "Blessed are the poor in spirit, for theirs is the kingdom of heaven."

This material had to be prepared—prepared, by conversion and temptation and suffering, for the moral state required by the builder of this kingdom. Hence, the builder himself taught them, not only by rules for real life and godliness, but by his personal example in temptation and suffering, whereby, they following him, were to be perfectly adapted to the end of their election. The sum of his spiritual code was love to God and our fellow-man, which he himself illustrated by a life worshipful and benevolent, and by patient submission to the will of his Father in heaven. He broadened their views of duty by showing that their sympathies and labors were to be co-extensive with the divine interest and love which   wide as the world itself.

And he began the work of construction by ,   the hearts and minds of his few followers on great, general principles of universal application, which was to be the model of construction, under the guidance of the Spirit, unto the end of time and unto the ends of the earth.

In order to establish his authority for this selection and preparation of material, and for this work of recon- struction of the human race on principles above those involved in the relations of family, and business, and society and human government, he performed works that no man could do, the crowning one of which was his own resurrection from the dead and ascension to the glory which he had enjoyed with the Father-worker before the world was ushered into creation. At his ascension he sent out his fellow-workmen to gather in "lively stones" for this spiritual house of the Lord. And some of the most gifted of them expounded it broadly, in the light of the divine purposes and pre- destinations, the offices of the persons of the Godhead, the theocracies and theophanies vouchsafed in the past, the laws and ordinations, the promises, prophecies and providences recorded in the sacred Scriptures, but specially, in the light of the great instrument of its erection, "the wisdom of God and the power of God." One of these workmen frequently refers to the work in such express terms as "ye are God's building," "ye are no more strangers and foreigners, but fellow-citizens with the saints and of the household of God, and are built upon the foundatio.   he apostles and prophets, Christ himself bei... ue chief corner-stone, in whom all the building fitly framed together groweth unto an holy temple in the Lord, in whom ye also are builded together for an habitation of God through the Spirit."—Eph. ii. 19–22. And another has given a gorgeous delineation of its laborious upbuilding on earth and triumphal completion in heaven.

But the Master Builder did not go from the earth until he had promised his faithful workmen, "And lo, I am with you alway, even unto the consummation of the age."

3

CHAPTER VI.

IN NATURE.

All in all.—1 Cor. xv. 28.

THE τέκτων of earth was the τέκτων of heaven, by whom are all things that are made in heaven and in earth. In this universal edification were involved purpose, plan, principles and phenomena. This implies that there was a period when there was no existence except the divine. The pantheist who involves the idea of Deity in the works of nature, denies this, as do other deists who hold to the eternity of matter. But logically and chronologically the rest of the universe may be stripped away from the divine existence, and the great I Am stand alone in the glory and triplicity of his being—living in the blessedness and excellence of his own conscious and cogitating and sentient being. In this being, Father, Son and Holy Spirit, there was formed, at some period in the distant past, with regard to a widespread nature—physical and metaphysical—a definite purpose.

THE PURPOSE.

The purpose was that the divine being should not be alone in the universe, that there should be other existences, material and immaterial; and that these objects should be so impressed with the attributes of the divine

34

nature that the intelligence created in the image of the divine nature should apprehend these attributes and thus learn the nature of the self-existent, everlasting and creative God. This was the end of creation; for there could be no greater good to the creature than the knowledge of the creator, the contemplation of whom would elevate him more and more into the likeness of Divinity. These attributes were to be reflected in nature, physical and metaphysical. But there is much in the divine being which cannot be known by mental observation and excogitation. There is much that can be known only by experience, and much by the experience of what is not blessed, but distressing and evil. Love can be known only by experience of love, and the comfort of mercy and grace only by the experience of sorrow and guilt. It was in the divine purpose, therefore, that moral evil should be permitted to enter the universe to the end that his mercy and grace might be exhibited and experienced in deliverance therefrom. Thus it was that his vast purpose of creation compassed not only the creation but the re-creation of the world. In the purpose there was unity in the will of the Trinity, who were to be engaged unitedly and severally in the execution. Whether there was any period of duration in the purposing, or whether any period elapsed between the purpose and the plan, who among the creatures of God can tell?

THE PLAN.

The plan of the universe was of a two-fold character —it was to be essential and phenomenal. As to essential nature, the will of God with regard to the universe was so fixed that it might be defined by the name of order or law, relating to light and sound, and heat and cold, and cohesion and repulsion, and gravity and electricity, and all the rest comprehended in what man calls physical science; and this divine will or order was to hold perpetually, and to permeate in every direction necessary for the support and continuance of the most varied and the most useful constitution of things. And these essential principles were to be one of the objects of human search and investigation, in order to the edification of human nature. This system of order or law may be conceived as apart from the phenomena by which it is expressed, as a system far-reaching, complex and perfect; just as the nervous system of the human body may be conceived in the image of the body, yet as something complete in the conception as apart from the body. In this essential part of the ideal was comprehended every event possible in the physical universe in every department, so long as the physical universe should last.

But as the spirit distinct from the body is clothed upon with flesh and bone and sinew, as an encasement as well as an exponent and index, so this system of essences was represented by the outward things of nature in the various forms of matter, more or less gross and endless in variety, as land and water, and wood and metal, and wind and gas, and a countless number of substances compassed in the kingdoms of matter, brute, vegetable, animal, human, angelic. These phenomena were designed for the immediate observation and use of the intelligent creature to be made, who should have senses as well as mental and moral powers, and to these senses these phenomena were to be addressed for profit and for pleasure.

In this plan intelligent beings were to be created, who themselves should be in the image of God and who should not only study themselves for the discovery of God, but should study all of his works, obvious and latent, even to the remotest principles, that he might be known and adored.

And such was to be the relation between this intelligent creation and the lower orders of creation, over which the higher order was to rule, that the fate of the higher should be the fate of the lower. This may be illustrated in man : if he stands in the image of his maker, the whole world should be full of the divine glory; if he falls, the world around him should fall. He is the representative of a race and of the house of the race, and on his weal or woe depends that of the represented world. This was the divine plan for wise purposes. But man would fall. This was contemplated in the original purpose. And the most important part of the plan was, that God himself should become manifest in the human image of himself, and by a history on earth of wondrous kind, work out in the eyes of the intelligent universe a restoration far exceeding the original creation and far more reflective of the deep nature of God. Thus by the transactions of the τέκτων among men the nature of God should be made more perfectly known to the uttermost limits of the intelligent universe, which, as has been said, was the purpose of the world's creation. "God created all things by Jesus Christ to the intent that now unto the principalities and powers in heavenly places might be known by the Church the manifold wisdom of God, according to the eternal purpose, which was purposed in Christ Jesus our Lord . . . of whom the whole family in heaven and earth is named."

Here was the ideal essential and phenomenal before the great architect of the universe, perfect, practical, wide-spread, glorifying, and committed to his Son for execution.

THE CONSTRUCTION.

Such is the omnipotent power of the $\tau\acute{\epsilon}\kappa\tau\omega\nu$ that he might, by a single word, have brought into existence and constructed the whole wide-spread universe. Of this we have positive proof. When on earth he brought by a word the dead to life. And in the beginning he spake and there was light, and he spake and the water and the land were separated. But the end of creation must never be forgotten, viz., the revelation of the divine nature. Hence the work is more gradual and divided into parts, that the human mind might apprehend and appreciate, and thus the impression with regard to the Creator be deeper, clearer, and more lasting. Hence we see $\acute{o}\ \tau\acute{\epsilon}\kappa\tau\omega\nu$ bringing the rough material of the physical universe out of nothing. That is a wonder the more wonderful as it is considered. Too wonderful is it for the modern Christian scientist, who, wishing to adjust this fact of creation to a primal law of physical science, *ex nihilo nihil fit,* holds that there is an externity of the divine nature as well as an internity, from which all material creation was derived without violation of this physical postulate. But man need not be more careful of the divine honor than is God himself. Enough that God created the material for the universe. And all the parts of each work are put together so perfectly on the principles involved that they are at once harmonious, unified, and perpetually united. And may not the creation of our planet be the model for all worlds? Thus worlds are united to worlds, and systems to systems, into a harmonious and unified and perpetual universe for the reflection of God and the manifestation of his nature.

On our globe man, in the image of God, is created—man dual, male and female, in representation of the persons of the Godhead and the creative power of God. Man is put there, as lord of all the lower creations, which is the best representation of the Lord of Glory.

Thus the natural attributes of Deity are represented in the physical, and the mental and moral in the human creation, of the grand universe constructed according to an eternal purpose and plan of the τέκτων of the Gospel.

But man thus created supposes society and government, art and science, varied knowledge and experience; and the realization of all these accessories of his being is wrapped up, either in himself or in nature around him ; so that he need lack nothing, with proper exercise of gifts afforded, to penetrate the recesses of this wonderful construction, physical and metaphysical—natural and spiritual—constructed for him by the creative and merciful Master Builder of all.

But this construction of nature must be looked into more in detail, as a reflector of the divine nature. Look, for a moment, into

I. Insensate nature—its laws and substances as presented in the sciences.

(1.) Take the exact science of mathematics as underlying and pervading all the rest. Through the whole of this science, from the multiplication table to the calculus, there is the all-pervading principle that there is no possibility of solution of problem, or demonstration of proposition, without the most absolute accuracy. The slightest deviation in number or matter defeats the desired result. This principle pervades not only pure and abstract mathematics, but it holds good in all the applications of mathematics to other sciences of physics or of business, whether chemistry or astronomy, whether commerce or mechanics. In fact, it pervades all the departments of nature, not only physical but also metaphysical, moral and spiritual. Now, what could illustrate more perfectly than this the absolute rectitude of the Creator of all? It indicates that his being is inconsistent with the least error or wrong. He is and must be absolutely perfect as to the rightness of his nature. When Pythagoras based creation on numbers, he presented only a symbolic truth of the universe being founded on the absolute and eternal rectitude of its Creator, which is everywhere displayed in the all-pervading laws of exact mathematics.

(2.) Take the sciences of botany and natural history. The flora and fauna of millions of variety, scattered promiscuously and with apparent infinite confusion over the surface of the earth, are by these sciences collected into a comparatively few genuses and species, so that what seems "confusion worst confounded," is reduced to perfect order. How strikingly does this indicate the perfect system and order of the divine government, which has every event classified and labelled and serving its pre-ordained mission in the accomplishment of the great purpose of creation, notwithstanding the events of history and the circumstances of life seem to be haphazard and confused and incapable of any orderly classification. 'O τέχτων gives us a picture of the truth of his universal government, despite the appearances to the contrary, in these sciences of botany and natural history, as in other sciences of man.

(3.) Take the science of geology. Take the fact of the hundreds of millions of years through which our globe has been forming by the accretion of particles. This globe is one of the least and perhaps one of the youngest of worlds. What, then, the greatest and the oldest as to their gradual formation? How suggestive of the age of the τέχτων. And what a picture does it afford of the divine patience and, hence, of all the passive qualities of Deity. How could the enduring and long-suffering Spirit of the great Maker of all be more perfectly represented? What may not be expected of his mercy, what of his wrath, what of the gradual accomplishment of all the purposes of his will?

(4.) Glance at mineralogy and meteorology, and what do we see?

(a.) The hidden metal and precious stone, so hard to find, so difficult to get, how well does it portray the deep things of God, which the unearnest never suspect, which only the most diligent, and those that have known the hammer and fire of severe experience, ever attain unto in any degree. But none shall ever see the whole of the divine nature.

(b.) Look at the mysteries of the wind, of the weather. None of these movements of nature is without obedience to law as fixed as the throne of God. Yet who can understand them? This was designed by the τέκτων in the structure of physical nature. It is the reply to the query, Who by searching can find out God, can find out God to perfection?

(5.) Take astronomy. Take the most phenomenal presentation of the lights of heaven bending over us everywhere and forever, and how could the great architect and builder have conceived and constructed anything more pictorially perfect of the divine omniscience and omnipresence and everlastingness? David was no astronomer and was not lost in the laws of attraction and repulsion, in the dimensions and distances, in the weight and reciprocal influences of worlds. He looked up with a child's eyes and sang, "The heavens declare the glory of God!" And in the results of these revolving spheres, as to day and night, the seasons of the year, the eclipses of each other, what side-pictures have we of the truths of life and death, of the divine care and benevolence, and of the folly of judgment by mere appearance of things!

II.   Glance now at the construction and constitution of animal, human, and angelic nature.

(1.) See in the gradation of life from the animalcule to the arch-angel what the distance between the highest creature and the Son of the Creator!

(2.) See in the universal distinctions, the all-pervading law of life from death, and learn of the eternally decreed sacrifice of the τέκτων and the eternity of ruin as a means of an everlasting life!   Devils gave the most powerful testimony of the Godship of the Carpenter's Son!

(3.) See how near is Lucifer to Gabriel, the devil to the angel, and tremble for self and for the τέκτων on the mount of temptation!   Think not of heaven as an eternal and inevitable incarceration in bliss, whence there is no possible outgoing unto evil, but as a state of moral fixedness to do and be the will of the great ἀρχιτέκτων.

III.   Look at the plan of nature as a whole.   Consider it in its origin as a perfect mirror of the great Maker; deplore sin as the tarnisher of this great revelation, yet learn from it of God, as we may, and rejoice at the prospect of its future restoration and its perfect and eternal revelation of the creator and preserver of all, to the glory of the Son, "from whom and unto whom are all things and by whom all things consist."

CHAPTER VII.

IN THE BIBLE.

These are they which testify of me.—John v. 39.

IN the Scriptures many are the hidden things of this being; hence the command, "Search the Scriptures." The earth and the sea combined are not more full of treasures than the oracles of God are of "the truth as it is in Jesus." But while we are to search for him, as for silver and gold, how obviously is he seen in many parts, yea, in every department of the world. Who walked and talked with the first man and woman in "the cool of the day" in Eden? Who was predicted as the bruiser of the serpent's head? Of whom was Noah a symbol, and who was it that "preached to the spirits in prison" in the days of Noah? Was he not the seed of whom the promise to Abraham was given? And who was it that appeared to Joshua on the plains of Jericho, and to Manoah the parent of the giant Samson? I need not recall the I Am in the burning bush of Midian, the Messiah of the Psalms of David, and of the predictions of the prophets. In the New Testament who else is seen by the eye of faith, from Matthew to Revelation, but the τέκτων of whom all the Scriptures, in every part and of every age, clearly testify?

And the same spirit of grace and severity that

44

marked his personal character, and the same end of restoring the right relations between God and man, are they not everywhere apparent throughout the word binding, as by silver cords, its varied parts into one great whole?

And wonderful is this divine work of which ὁ τέκτων is not only the subject but the constructor. Wonderful is the Master Builder's construction in nature, but more wonderful is it in the Bible. It is more wonderful:

1st. Because while in the former the whole construction is under his hand alone, and his mind and spirit are naturally impressed on the work of his own hand, in the latter he works through others, in different ages and of different degrees of moral and mental character, and yet he makes this structure a perfect representation of the Creator.

2d. Because the representation in this structure relates to the being of God, more mysterious and more gracious, and more essential than in that of nature. It is a more advanced—a higher revelation of Deity, and not less symmetrical, and harmonious and unified than the construction of nature.

And let it be remarked, that a more certain knowledge of this work may be acquired than that of nature. For the facts and exposition of nature we have to depend upon men, like ourselves, imperfect. For the truths of the Bible we may rely upon the author himself.

In the examination of any building or institution, or commodity, it is not needful, in order to have a true conception of its plan, its genius or its character, to do more than to examine component parts of it. Thus let us see, from samples taken here and there from the Bible, how perfectly it represents the Creator in his Son, the beginning and the ending of this revelation. •

1. We enter the book in about the middle of it, and we hear of one to be the son of a virgin. Nothing seems more improbable. But seven hundred years after, the Carpenter's Son himself appears, the divinely attested Son of the Virgin Mary. Here is a thread in this fabric running through centuries and connecting the revelation of these centuries.

2. Again we read of a man brought as a lamb to the slaughter. This is marvellous, in Judea where human sacrifice was an abomination. But hundreds of years after, the Spirit of God bids one of his builders to expound this history, and it is written, " Beginning at this Scripture, Philip preached unto him, Jesus." Here is another thread of the same sort consorting with the other, and running through the ages.

3. But what is this ritual of blood running through the Jewish economy, and going back before the flood to the first family of the human race? All through this worship, and through all worship, blood, blood, blood. How strange! Who will explain this in the Bible revelation? John, a chief builder of God explains. Seeing the Carpenter's Son coming towards him he cries, " Behold the Lamb of God that taketh away the sin of the world! " Here the very extremes of the

Scripture structure are bound together by this revelation of the Carpenter's Son.

4. How strange that the angel of death should not visit the Hebrew homes in Egypt, whose door-posts were besprinkled with blood. But how plain when we read, " Christ our Passover is sacrificed for us."

5. That story of Jonah in the whale's belly and his escape, how it mystified the ages, but how striking and useful as expounded by the Carpenter's Son himself, as representing his own imprisonment in the bowels of the earth for three days, and the great deliverance of his resurrection !

6. But why go into detail? Hear the τέκτων with regard to himself and this construction, "Search the Scriptures . . . for these are they that testify of me." And in order to make plainness more plain he illustrates the fact that the Scriptures are constructed for the revelation of God in the face of Jesus Christ his Son, by a general exposition of the Bible of which we have this divinely authorized statement, "Beginning at Moses and all the prophets, he expounded unto them in all the Scriptures the things concerning himself."

And what are the things in all the Scriptures concerning the τέκτων ? They are the hidden things of God not revealed in nature—more than his omnipotence and his eternity, they are the things relating to his eternal purposes of grace which are only hinted at in nature, which were gradually taught in the older Scriptures, but which culminated in the earthly life and death, and resurrection and ascension of the Carpenter's Son, of which we shall see more fully hereafter. Suffice it now that the τέχτων in the Bible, so unique, so complete, so harmonious, so perfect and so wonderfully preserved, while the works of man's hands are commonly destroyed, is one of the greatest wonders of the universe.

But, though superior to nature, how like nature as a structure is this Bible?

1st. The whole structure is based on principles as in nature, so well defined and so uniform, that these principles may be and have been, collected in a science, like any natural science, which is called a System of Divinity or Theology.

2d. These principles, like those of nature, are expressed in phenomena of history, individual and national, human and angelic, natural and spiritual; of poetry and prophecy, of the most varied and divine sort; of doctrine didactic and illustrative, relating to the past, the present and the future; and of symbols without number concerning the human and the divine, the temporal and the eternal. Take the phenomena of nature and compare them with those of revelation, and they will not be found more striking and more representative of the principles on which they are founded.

3d. If it be held that nature is evolved from a particle by the power of omnipotence, what a world of truth does the Bible present as the fruit of the germ-principle, "the seed of the woman shall bruise the head of the serpent!"

The sun of nature comes and goes, and may some day sink into everlasting night. But the central light of this structure is the Sun of Righteousness, whose rays ever shine the same, and which shall be in meridian glory when the glory of nature with its sun and moon, and stars shall roll up as a scroll and pass away with a great noise. The principles and structure of nature are temporal, the truths and facts of the Bible are eternal. Angels live above the things of our nature, but they bend their minds to pry into the things in this construction of the Carpenter's Son. We know not of what is called heaven, but of what we do know, there is nothing higher, nothing broader, nothing deeper, nothing more full of glory and of love, than this last and most complete work of the τέκτων, which we call, by way of eminence, The Bible.

Let it be added, that this work of the τέκτων, like his other great works, such as physical and human nature, and the experiences of grace, though but a part of the great Universal Temple of truth and of fact that he is rearing, is like each of these great works represented as if a temple itself. As the complete chapels under the dome of St. Peter's Cathedral, so are these grand works, little temples in the universal and eternal house of his hand. David's conception of nature is as "the handiwork of God—a Temple for the sun;" and of spiritual worship, "dwelling in the house of the Lord forever." The Carpenter's Son spoke of his body as "this temple;" and Paul says of the church, "Whose house are we, if we hold fast the confidence

4

and the rejoicing of the hope firm unto the end."
Under the same view is God's Word commonly held.
A learned professor catching the figure from the Word
itself says, "The Bible is a grand whole—a Temple
whose parts are harmonious, whose symmetry is sublime,
whose finish is divinely perfect, and whose infinite
spaciousness is filled with the praises of God." Is not
this the structure of which Solomon says, "Wisdom
hath builded her house, she hath hewn out her seven
pillars, she hath killed her beasts, she hath mingled her
wine, she hath also furnished her table, she hath sent
forth her maidens, she crieth upon the highest places of
the city, Whoso is simple let him turn in hither; as for
him that wanteth understanding, she saith to him,
Come eat of my bread and drink of the wine which I
have mingled. Forsake the foolish and live, and go
in the way of understanding . . . The fear of
the Lord is the beginning of wisdom, and the knowledge of the Holy is understanding." I need not
repeat that this wisdom is ὁ τέκτων, the Alpha and the
Omega of Divine Revelation.

CHAPTER VIII.

IN PROVIDENCE AND HISTORY.

The very hairs of your head are all numbered.—Matt. **x**. 30.

PROVIDENCE is that divine care over the works of his hand, sometimes natural, sometimes supernatural, which God bestows in all ages of the world, through the agency of the second person of the Godhead, and which was abundantly illustrated in the history of Israel—individual and national. It is not strange that many hold that the world and the inhabitants and interests thereof are put under a reign of law; and that that law, applied or submitted to by human intelligence, is sufficient for the conduct of human affairs; as submission to such law by animal and insensate nature suffices for the stability and prosperity of the material and animal world. Thus it seems to science. But this is not the exposition of the divine government, as given in the divine word and illustrated in a part of the world's history. It was not natural law that brought the world into being, and it is not natural law that preserves it and provides for all its changes by divine wrath or grace, and adapts it specially to the divine purposes. Was it natural law that flooded the earth and then ran off the waters of the deluge? Was it natural law that divided the waters of the Red Sea and of Jordan for the passage of the children of Israel? Was it natural law that stopped

51

the sun over Gibeon and the moon over Ajalon, that Joshua might avenge himself upon the enemies of his people and of his people's God? And who was the divine agent of this superintending rule? Who was the I Am that conducted the Hebrews by the pillar of cloud and of fire from Egypt to the land of promise? Who was the Angel of the Covenant with whom Jacob wrestled until the break of day and would not let go until he blessed him? Who was he "like unto the Son of God" that stood with the Hebrew children in the fiery furnace of Nebuchadnezzar? The Jehovah of the Old Testament is the Jesus of the New, who said plainly, "Before Abraham was I Am."

Nor is this superintendence less divine when conducted by means according to natural law than when by means above that law. What superintendence could be more providential than that over Joseph in the court of Pharaoh, and Esther in the court of Ahasuerus, or that over Philip when he met and preached to the African Jewish proselyte, and Paul in his missionary tours among the Gentiles?

And the providence of the past is the providence of the present—the same agent, the same methods, (except perhaps the miraculous), the same end. Nor does it relate to merely the great events of history. He who numbers the hairs of the head, who notes the sparrow's fall, who feeds the bird of the air without barn, clothes the flower of the field without its spinning or weaving, is not unmindful of the humblest of the children of men, into whose hands and brains he puts the means of support and of progress and of prosperity. He that drove the plane and plied the hammer on the carpenter's bench of Nazareth, stands now by the artisan and mechanic and manufacturer and every workman of every sort and grade of our own day. He is the workman's best friend, best counsellor, best support. But, unlike the bird of the air, the beast of the field, the workman is free, which makes him a man; and this freedom of will determines whether the friendship and counsel and support of the Master Builder shall be received. Wise would it be for Knights of Labor, and laborers not Knights, to recognize and act upon this vital element in the history of human crafts. But, whether this Master Builder is recognized or not, he does not permit the will or the wilfulness of man to interfere with the great purposes for which he controls the history of the world. And is not this general principle of divine providence applicable to all of the affairs of men? He who when on earth had his eye on the shepherd with his flock, the vine-dresser with his vines, and the tiller of the soil sowing his seed and reaping his harvest, and the merchantman with his varied commodities, from each of whom he derived striking illustrations for the elucidation of his doctrines; he who had to do with the government officer at the receipt of custom, and had debates with lawyers and philosophers and religionists of every sort, and who was not indifferent with regard to the rule of the rulers of Palestine and the king at Rome; this one who noticed the children piping and dancing in the streets, and enjoyed the hospitalities of Cana and Bethany, surely he is not neglectful of any human interests, material, professional, religious, social or governmental. And has this not been so from the beginning? Was he not with the first shepherd who brought to the altar a more acceptable offering than his brother, and with the first tiller of the soil, to whom he said, "If thou doest not well sin lieth at thy door"? And who was the instructor of Jubal, "the father of all that handle the harp and the organ;" and of Tubal Cain, who was the "instructor of every artificer in iron and brass"? Did he not lay the foundations of all government in the family institution; and has he not supervised to check or to stimulate all the governments of men, whether patriarchal, monarchical, despotic or democratic, as he has been interested in all the great systems of philosophy or religion, all of which either represent some truth of nature or celebrate some attribute of the ἀρχιτέκτων himself? In his day, I may add, he had to do also with the man of blood, the Roman soldier, and recently there has issued from the press an admirable work, illustrative of his presence now in the scenes of war, named "Christ in the Camp." In fact, the trades, and vocations, and professions, and customs, and societies, and governments, and wars even of men, are the methods, with or without human acquiescence to his will, by which the great builder of human history carries on the progress of the world. Man, with all his faculties, and susceptibilities and volition, is just as much the instrument of the ἀρχιτέκτων of the universe as the laws of gravitation and cohesion, or the laws of the earth's revolution and fructifying power. God is omnipotent. This is hard to realize. But it is true. And with omnipotence it is as easy to rule the free agency of man and of devils as it is to rule the brute matter of the earth. And part of the divine providential government is to accomplish its sovereign purpose by letting men and devils do their own will. The grandest accomplishments of Jehovah were wrought out by man's first defiance of the divine will and the diabolical execution of his Son on the cross of Calvary. The sovereign τέκτων does not propose to feed any creatures of his hand with the breath of life or clothe them with the garbs of flesh or of spirit without using them for the achievement of his own supreme glory. If the Divine Maker ever annihilates a creature it will be when he cannot control him for the accomplishment of his eternal purposes. That will not be world without end !

But we must not forget his own personal labors of mind and of spirit, which bring him in sympathy with all the toils and struggles of human intellects and souls, over which he has also a minute superintendence. Socrates said he was constantly followed by a good demon giving him counsel, and the same might have said Plato, and Aristotle, and Bacon, and Locke, and Newton; and thus might say to-day every child of mental toil and agony. Matthew says angels came and ministered unto the Carpenter's Son in his conflicts and passion. But more than an angel, the Carpenter's Son himself, made perfect by his own suffering, ministers to every earnest child of heart-labor and head-toil. Thus he supervises and superintends by his providence not only the material and circumstantial, but the intellectual and moral interests of the world, fitting or over-ruling all for the construction of his great and universal structure of praise and glory.

If it be said that this divine guidance does not appear commonly in the historic records of human events, I ask, What is the essential difference between the records of history sacred and profane? The answer may be given in the statement of a case. Suppose a merely human historian had given the account of Moses conducting the Hebrews through the wilderness, would there have been seen anything of the divine hand? Has not the greatest of Roman historians done this, and does he not attribute to wild asses what Moses attributes to the providence of God? And suppose the rise and fall of the Assyrian and Egyptian powers, or the powers of Greece and Rome, had been written by the pens of Moses or of John, would not the hand of God have been as apparent as in the history of ancient Israel, or of the early church? The essential difference between these two classes of history is that sacred history records from the standpoint of the great first cause, while profane history records from the standpoint of second causes. Were the history of America written by the pen of Luke its discovery by Columbus, the struggles of the colonies, the Constitution of the United States, the conflict between the States, the development of boundless resources, the progress of the truth, as well as the earthquake, the tempests and floods, and the wide-spread evils of the land, would be seen connected with the divine rule, just as much as in the history of the discovery, the settlement, the tribe-troubles, the blessings and the cursings of the land of Canaan, given according to promise to the children of Abraham. Was not Jehovah as much the God of Moab as of Judah? Is he not as much the God of the Caucasian race, or of the Asiatic, or African race, as of the race of Abram? Are not the nations of the earth the children of Adam, the son of God? And does not "the only begotten Son" of the Father of all, whose mediation and sacrifice is the providential reason for the preservation of any of the children of men, superintend these nations of the earth as certainly as he did the tribes of Israel? Jehovah is a broad God—he is the God universal, not merely the God of the Jew or of the Christian. The difference in his dealing with the races and nations of men, as respects his connection with their history, is merely seeming; it is merely in the fact that he writes the history of some peoples and man writes the history of others. But does he not write some history—the history in the Scriptures—to teach us the laws by which all history should be written or interpreted? Take the histories of Herodotus, Livy, Xenophon, Gibbon, Macaulay, Bancroft, and apply to them the law of interpretation derived from the history of Israel and of the early Christians, and so far as the statements of these histories are true, they would read just as sacred history reads, and many of the events would appear just as wonderful as the most marvellous events of inspired history.

But what is history? Some one says, "Philosophy
teaching by example." Is it not even in its narrowest
sense more than this? Is it not the record of God's
dealing with his creatures, whether the record recognizes
the hand of God or not? But this definition relates
merely to the record of the world's events. May not
history be taken in the broad sense of the consecution of
these events, whether they be recorded or not? How
little of the events of the universe is recorded. Even
on earth, what is recorded of the changes, the growth
the progress, the experience, the acts of things and persons, is as nothing in comparison with the endless
unwritten volumes on hidden pages, locked up in the
arcana of physical and animal nature and in the bosom
of mysterious and self-ignorant mankind. And elevat-
ing and widening the range of vision, taking in the
circuit of creation, with its countless worlds and its
endless grades of intelligence and morals, and the
unnumbered cycles of the existence of many; when we
look thus and ask the question, How much history is
there? we see that history is something more than the
sparse and partial records of the human historian. The
records of all these worlds' experience and acts and possessions may be made on the minds and memories of
recording angels. We know not. But we know that
there is a record of every atom, and relation, and change,
and event, and experience, and thought, and sensation,
and purpose, and hope, and possibility, that has ever
existed in heaven, in earth, in hell, in any and in every
part of the universe, and that is in the mind and heart

of the ἀρχιτέκτων of all. This record is clear and vast and capable of review. It is the photograph of history universal. To human mind, and perhaps angelic, this boundless history might seem as little more than chaos itself, which might be best represented by a huge blot upon the memory that contains it. But the picture of no tree, nor beautiful scene, is more distinctly depicted on the retina of the human eye, the recollection of no happy event of yesterday in personal history, is clearer to the memory that cherishes and reviews it hourly, than is the whole history, in every minutiæ and detail from the beginning until now, depicted on the mind of the omniscient and unfailing τέκτων. Nor is this panoramic. The review requires not a second's time. It is all present in one unbroken view in his eternal now. It is a photograph as the photograph of some picture gallery in the palace of a great king.

But how can there be a photograph of the united events and experiences of the universe as a picture gallery, or a palace of many departments, unless those events and experiences are united, and form in fact a great whole, as the gallery or the palace? Here is suggested again the constructiveness of the great τέκτων which is universal and everlasting. The relations and ideas, and events and experiences of creation are realities as much as the material of the earth or the sun. They are as capable of unification and of construction as are the parts of a throne, a palace, a temple. And thus is all history upbuilt before the mind and by the hand of the universal ἀρχιτέκτων. There may be dis-

covered reason for this. This history is the fruitage of
the essences of creation. These are the works by which
all may be tested. The unified and constructed whole
may be needful for the divine vindication in the courts
of eternity, in the presence of the assembled intelligence and spirits of the universe. It may be needful
to give a vision of the whole to human or angelic gaze,
as the glory of the whole world was needlessly exhibited
to the Carpenter's Son. It may be that this constructed
history is as needful, for reasons unknown, as the construction of man, of the Bible, the earth, the universe.
The τέκτων implies construction, as the essence of his
powers, and the circumstantial and invisible things
of the universe fall under that power as all things
visible. And this history, universal and constructed,
involves the immediate presence and superintendence of
the great constructor, the Carpenter's Son. And let it
be said that this great structure of universal history
is only another department of that universal Temple
toward the completion of which all things tend, which
reminds us of the words of the Carpenter's Son, " In
my Father's house are many mansions."

But there is a view of this subject without which
this consideration of it would be fatally defective. The
divine τέκτων is building up his universal Temple for
the eternal praise of his name, by the preservation and
progress of the worlds, through material and immaterial works, and powers, and governments, and events
and histories over which he exercises a providential
care, without which no reign of law could prevent for

one second a reign of universal chaos. But while he superintends all for this vast ultimate purpose, he superintends it, as he himself declares, for the benefit of the heirs of eternal glory, to whose history he must and does give a special and effectual supervision and superintendence. The specialness of it is because of its effectiveness. The ways of these heirs are wisdom's ways, and lead inevitably to their predestined glory. Hence, the superintendence of all else has reference in part to their universal aiding to the accomplishment of the destiny of the children of light. Do not the devils even promote their glory? We know that the angels of glory do, for thus is it written. And is it not further written that all things work together for the good of those predestined to conformity to the image of the Son of God? And the consummation of this great end of divine providence will be one of the grand pillars in the universal and eternal Temple erecting by the Carpenter's Son.

CHAPTER IX.

IN THE PURPOSES OF GRACE.

He hath chosen us in him before the foundation of the world.—Eph. i. 4.

THE foregoing, with regard to the Carpenter's Son, have been glimpses of him from the several standpoints which the treatment of the subject required to be taken. But now a more connected view will be given, comprehending many of these partial views, but more comprehensive than any of them. I propose to sketch him briefly from his seat in the Eternal Council of grace to the execution of the redemptive purpose of this Council in his state of resumed glory.

PRELIMINARY QUESTIONS.

It has been said that all things were made for the glory of God, and all things were permitted or ordered to be done for the same end. In the Revelation of Divine Truth we have a glimpse of the universe before the introduction of moral evil. This glimpse is given in the statement of the occasion of its introduction in the undue self-elevation of a lofty spirit near the throne of God. Before that self-elevation this spirit was lofty in his greatness and goodness, and so were kindred spirits, and the universe was full of the good and the blessed and the glorious only. The earth, before the fall of man, of which we have a picture, may be fairly

62

regarded a miniature of the beauty and the blessedness of that broader state which characterized the creatures and creation of the Great Maker and Architect of all. And suppose the mind capable of taking in this widespread universe as originally made before the introduction of evil. What a stupendous and magnificent and palatial Temple surrounding the throne of the Most High! Could not the universe remain so forever? Would not the glory and the blessedness of the Maker and Architect be complete and perpetual? But we must not forget our postulate that all existence, outside of the Divine Being, took its rise in the eternal purpose to reveal God to the eyes of intelligent creatures. And who shall say that the whole of the knowable being of God can be compassed in the knowledge and experience of what is good and great? Are there not unfathomable depths in his being of infinite holiness, and justice and wrath, that no exhibition of good and greatness and blessedness can disclose? And his eternal sovereignty, not to be questioned as the price of the continuance of the glory of creation and of the divine throne! Shall not that be revealed for the essential benefit of the universe, and how shall the revelation be made? God is not the author of moral evil. But does not the entrance of it in the form of rebellion, and the punishment of it in "everlasting chains under darkness," give the best conceivable exhibition of the infinite and ineffable sacredness of the absolute sovereignty of the Most High? We may deplore, and do deplore, as doubtless do the holy ones of the spirit-world who keep their first estate. But the permission of evil was wise though utterly mysterious and incomprehensible, and may it not have been the origin of the greatest of all revelations of the Eternal Maker—the revelation of the infinite grace of his being? In passing, it may be asked whether the ancient and philosophic notion of light springing out of darkness, of good coming out of evil, had its origin in some surmise or glimpse of this mystic eternal truth, of the exhibition of the mercy and grace of God, arising from the exhibition of his eternal wrath?

And another question of the dark and mysterious things of the world. Did the death which is said to have reigned on our planet before the creation of man have connection with the original introduction and penalty of moral evil? One of three things seems to be true. Either the fall of man had an anticipatory effect in the ruin of creatures before his creation, or the reign of death which pervaded the pre-Adamic world was a fell consequence of the fall of the angelic race of transgressors, who must have had some connection with our world, or there may be suffering and death where there is no transgression. The first view has some analogy in the fact that the effects of redemption extend beyond the race of man in another sphere, for if redemption may go beyond the race redeemed in the future, may not the fall have gone before the sinner in the past? The second view receives some likelihood from the fact, already mentioned, of the intense interest that the angelic race has shown in our world,—though not manifested, as some hold, in "the sons of God" even visiting it and becoming allied, in the early ages, with "the daughters of men." With regard to the last view there seems to be some support in the experience of man, and of the Carpenter's Son himself, both of whom have endured extreme sorrow in the exercise of the holiest affection of their being. But an answer to this question is not needful for our present purpose, so we leave it among the unsolved, and perhaps unsolvable problems of this world of mysteries. The simple Bible reader without the influence of science, I should add, may deny the premise that death did reign before the fall of man, and that settles the question conclusively to his mind. This denial makes our world originally made for man and its whole destiny, for weal or woe, to depend alone upon his fate by the fall or by the scheme for his personal redemption.

Here arises the question as to the Council of the Godhead with regard to the redemptive scheme for man. Did this Council succeed or antedate the introduction of moral evil? This is not a vain inquiry; our fuller compass of that scheme may depend upon the right answer to it. The intimations of revelation are that moral evil came first. That moral evil gave at once the occasion for one great revelation of the divine nature. But that revelation having been made, the redemptive scheme for another race, planned in the Council of the Trinity, gives another and greater revelation of the Almighty—the glory of which revelation has an important, if not essential, back-ground in the

5

previous exhibition of the eternal wrath that followed the violation of the divine will and rebellion against the supreme government of God. Hence, perhaps, the keen interest which the sons of God took in the creation of our physical world—the theatre of this exhibition of the divine grace; hence, perhaps their seeking, as we are told, to unravel the sacred and eternal mystery. And are we not distinctly informed that this scheme is for the instruction of "the principalities and powers in heavenly places," who had only known of wrath in connection with violated law? Thus this scheme of grace has a bearing far beyond the race and destiny of man, and is perhaps the grandest and completest revelation of Deity that ever has or ever will be made. This may be, and probably is, the ultimate revelation of God for which all creation was brought into being.

And here enters another question of eternal chronology —if the terms are not contradictory—whether the purpose to create the physical world succeeded or antedated the purposes of grace? If this purpose of creation succeeded the Counsels of Grace, as reason would seem to suggest, and as revelation seems to teach, by the creation of our earth and its surroundings actually following the purpose of redemption, the one being in time and the other in eternity, then have we the well-founded hypothesis that this whole material universe is a surrounding of the Cross of Christ which is to shed upon it its greatest and most enduring lustre. Many are the divine attributes reflected in the material world which declare so plainly the glory for which it was made, but the light of divine grace shed upon these reflections, gives them an additional significance which is their perfecting excellence. Not only do they exhibit divine omnipotence and omniscience and wisdom, but they exhibit these as the handmaids of divine love and mercy. Hence the universal Temple of creation is represented as resounding with acclaims not only of the redeemed but of the angelic hosts saying, " Blessing and glory, and power and dominion be unto him that sitteth upon the throne, and the Lamb forever and ever!" And here we see a confirmation of the view that the original conception of creation, in the Divine mind, was that of an infinite and eternal Temple to his praise, which is an outward exhibition of the inner and eternal verity of his own infinite and everlasting Temple-like being.

ETERNAL COUNCIL OF GRACE.

Angels had fallen and were lost forever, and thus the wrath of God would be eternally exhibited. Man shall be made in the image of God, and he shall fall by the machinations of the lost world, but shall he perish with the Devil? This fall may be the occasion, as has been said, of the profoundest revelation of the triune God; and hence the gracious purpose of the persons of the sacred Trinity who respectively and unitedly are to execute the plan. And in the very inception of the plan there is the revelation of the Trinity itself—three distinct persons in one eternal God. Had this revelation been made to the other intelligences? Was there need of the revelation either to the holy or the fallen race? Thus begins the grand purpose and plan of grace. But with the next step—the essence of the scheme—the atoning sacrifice of the Son, for the satisfaction of the divine government, comes the most unfathomable of mysteries. How shall God be vitally connected with man in a consciously personal being? How can the Divine mind suffer such personal association with sin which it has eternally punished in the angelic race? How could the human element of this being suffer and die, and the divine remain utterly unaffected? How could even the infinitude of divine grace submit to such a humiliation to save the guilty sinner, man? But the purpose that man as a race shall not die is formed; the plan for the salvation of the elect is complete. The Father fathers the scheme, the Spirit engages his efficient powers for its execution, the Son is the ready victim of the holy enterprise, for which mediatorial devotion he is to be crowned with mediatorial glories, world without end. But not only the victim is he to be. As the original agent of universal creation he is to be the Builder and Architect of the all-comprehending edifice of grace and glory, and hence he is to appear in the fulness of time as the Carpenter's Son.

But man is to be free. Suppose he refuse, after his voluntary fall, life eternal, as perhaps the devil did, is there no possibility of the failure of the scheme? God forbid! And forbidden was it in the eternal Council of Grace, "For whom he did foreknow he also did predestinate to be conformed to the image of his Son, . . . according to the eternal purpose which he purposed in Christ Jesus our Lord."

CHAPTER X.

IN MAN'S CREATION AND FALL.

CREATION.

Let us make man in our image.—Gen. i. 26.

THE abode in which he was settled, so beautiful, so varied, so vast, and fitted up with appliances so convenient, so magnificent, yea, so sublime, gave intimation of how excellent a being Adam was. And viewed in himself, so fair in person, so powerful in position, being duplex in nature and having constant communion with God, he stood among the grandest and most blessed of divine creations, and gave promise of being the head of a grand race worthy of "the image of God." Nor are we in this later dispensation left without exact representation of this good and great being. There is given us no personal image of the first man, but there is given the person whose image man originally was. He who appeared as the Carpenter's Son was the being who said, "Let us make man in our image," and who walked and talked with him in Eden. To know the first Adam in his excellence we have but to note the Second Adam in the mental, moral and spiritual attributes which he exhibited as he moved among the children of men, as "the brightness of the Father's glory and the express image of his person."

In several respects the first Adam excelled the second. He was made at once into the perfect image of the Son of God without passing through the formative period of infancy and childhood; he was not a burden-bearer, and stood erect in the strength of his untaxed and perfectly developed manhood; all his surroundings filled him with only profounder gladness of spirit and broader hope of life; and his meat and drink was to do the will, to receive the blessing and to imbibe the knowledge and wisdom and greatness of an unoffended God. Each day's creation added grandeur to the preceding glory of creation; but on the sixth day the wonderful series of created wonders culminated in the creation of man, the lord of all he was surrounded by, and of whose creation we have this record: "In the day that God created man, in the likeness of God created he him; male and female created he them, and blessed them and called their name Adam in the day when they were created." In order to represent perfectly the divine being as appeared in the Carpenter's Son, who embodied in himself all the attributes of humanity, the first Adam was made male and female. The two were one. "God called their name Adam." And as the federal head and representative of a great race to come, he was by way of eminence ὁ τέκτων γένους.

As an imperishable monument of creation a fixed period of time was set apart to celebrate the glory thereof; and that man, the centre of creation, was the chief glory of the works whose perpetual commemoration is secured by the revolving globe itself, have we not a suggestion in the holy seventh day being now divinely appointed as the memorial of the model of the first man, even the arisen Second Adam—a memorial to be sacredly recognized and honored as the price of prosperity personal and national?

And the glory of the two Adams is so interwoven that it is celebrated in a single song and exposition of inspiration, "What is man that thou art mindful of him? or the son of man that thou visitest him? Thou madest him a little lower than the angels; thou crownedst him with glory and honor, and didst set him over the works of thy hands. . . . But now we see not yet all things put under him. But we see Jesus, who was made a little lower than the angels for the suffering of death, crowned with glory and honor."

THE FALL.

In the day that thou eatest thereof thou shalt surely die.—Gen. ii. 1–17.

The fall of Adam is not invested with the difficulty that surrounds the fall of Satan. How a holy being, with his nature poised on the principle of supreme love to a sovereign God, can lose that poise by any movement of his own is hard to comprehend. Perhaps the jar was given to the holy angel from some power without, which had fallen before. But how did that power fall? This drives us quickly and inevitably into the ancient Persian idea of the co-eternity of the principles of good and evil. That solves the problem by overthrowing our own most radical conception of God as infinitely and eternally supreme. But no such insolvable difficulty enters into Adam's lapse and ruin. I hold in my hand a Copenhagen chronometer of the most perfect construction, and I drop into its delicate and complicated works a grain of sand. The whole mechanism is at once thrown into disorder, and the time-keeper becomes utterly unreliable as a keeper of time. Thus was it with the perfectly true and holy man and woman in the image of God. A disorganizing idea was dropped into their mental and moral structure by a power extraneous to itself. That fallen spirit who subtly approached the Carpenter's Son when on earth, approached the first Adam with exactly the same profoundly malicious and ingenious suggestion that he should be independent of the sovereign will of Jehovah. This had been his own fatally successful temptation, for it is written that through "pride" the Devil fell into condemnation. The Second Adam resisted the temptation by the word of God; but the profundity of the temptation to which Adam yielded was that the divine truth was questioned and denied and subverted in advance, and thus the protection of the divine word was laid aside by the temptation itself. There was wonderful wisdom in this, which the first Adam did not see as did the second. Hence, sin is described by the Carpenter's Son as the disbelief of him. The promised Spirit was to reprove the world "of sin because it hath not believed in me." The distrust of the Creator made a breach in the whole spiritual mechanism of the man, so that a flood-gate was open for every possible evil, and his ruin was so complete that it might be said of him as the Carpenter's

Son said of Satan, "I saw him fall from heaven like Lucifer!" If it be asked why Satan sought thus to ruin the first Adam, who was made lord of the lower creation, and the Second Adam, who was to recover the fallen position of the first, promising the one to make him like the gods and the other to give him the nations of the world without his contention for them, it may be asked in return, Was it because they were to hold the empire from which he had been dethroned, or was it merely because he is the Devil?

This virus of disbelief of God shot through the Adamic being, vitiating the whole of it, and cut him off from the controlling influence and power of the divine presence. He is left to himself. More than that, a flaming sword obstructs his way to the tree of life, which is a figure of the life-giving I Am, the full restoration to vital association with whom is described in the second Eden also as the tree of life, and the virtual restoration to which is described on earth in such gospel language as this, "For to me to live is Christ: Christ is formed within us the hope of glory." Thus was the sentence of death fully executed. No death could be more complete. The mere suspension of animation and being put into the grave would be no death to this death, living and perpetuated before the eyes of the universe. God's word was doubted; but the word of God was realized: "In the day that thou eatest thereof thou shalt surely die."

But the fall of man was not merely individual. Adam was the representative of a race on trial in its illustrious and God-like head. It was this relation, involving such momentous consequences, that made his creation the most elevated and the best protected from danger consistent with his necessary power of volition, and which made the test of loyalty the very simplest that could be given. But failing to abstain from the fruit of a single tree forbidden, while in possession of all the trees of Eden, and he and his race in him subsequently endorsing his disobedience as voluntary sin, he justly fell. The very earth itself fell, bringing forth thorns and briars instead of fruit and flowers. And how fearful the fall not only to his now self-conscious, guilty and God-fearing self, but to his posterity! His son was a fatricidal murderer, and a fugitive and vagabond on the face of the earth. And so corrupt became the family of man that "it repented God" that he had made him, and he washed the whole race, electing only eight souls, from the face of the earth. How fearful the picture of sin, the first race of transgressors in the waters of the deluge, the second in the fire of hell!

But why the election of eight souls? According to the eternal council, the human race—the image of God —is not to be destroyed. The living surety and future representative is already at hand on the outside of Eden. He avows man's final supremacy over the fell spirit that ruined him, in the unmistakable words, "The seed of the woman"—even himself—"shall bruise the head of the serpent." This must be through a conflict of blood; but it shall be. Yes, of blood! The blood is life, and life shall be given for life; but man, in his second representative, shall prevail and be restored. That is to be henceforth the grand programme of the whole world's history; for, for that was not the world made? Why then surprise at the universal flow of typical blood—blood for blood, blood for revenge, blood for the altar, blood staining and spreading over the whole world! This was the comfort and hope and virtual restoration in Adam's day, his son offering the lamb acceptable to God; and what but the same in our day? Since the self-offering of the Lamb of God, by the priestly hand of the Second Adam himself, where sin abounds grace much more abounds. So superabundant is divine grace that the cheering language with regard to the resurrection of the dead is, that, "As in Adam all die, so in Christ shall all be made alive." And more definite and circumstantial is the statement, "Wherefore as by one man sin entered into the world and death by sin, and so death passed upon all men, for that all have sinned; . . . therefore, as by the offence of one judgment came upon all men to condemnation, even so by the righteousness of one the free gift came upon all men unto justification of life."

CHAPTER XI.

IN PROGRESS OF REDEMPTIVE CONSTRUCTION.

ANTEDILUVIAN PERIOD.

Then began men to call upon the name of the Lord.—Gen. iv. 26.

THE start of this divine construction was fairly made in this period. Paul says that the church is built upon "the foundation of the apostles and prophets, Jesus Christ himself being the chief corner-stone." This corner-stone was virtually laid when the Lamb was slain from the foundation of the world; and there were many prophets and the greatest of apostles in this antediluvian period. This apostle was called sneeringly, in the gospel period, the Carpenter's Son; he was known, in the antediluvian period, under the name of Jehovah, which is rendered in our version of the Old Testament, THE LORD. Peter declares that this apostle, sent from heaven, preached before the flood. What did he preach? The great subject of his preaching might be inferred from the instruction given to the shepherd-son of the first man, with regard to the offering of the typical lamb. It may be more clearly discovered from the preaching of Noah, who is declared not only a just man and perfect in his generations, but a preacher of righteousness—of righteousness, not of the law which had been so fatally broken by Adam, and was so con-

76

demnatory and destructive in its effects; but the "righteousness which is by faith." What was the faith of that period? The faith of Abel and of Noah is put in the same category with the faith of Abraham and David, and theirs was the same faith as Peter's and John's, which "is the substance of things hoped for, the evidence of things not seen." In the antediluvian period, this faith may have looked back to the eternally slain lamb, which the first great apostle must have preached and expounded; and laying hold of his righteousness, to be afterwards mediatorially wrought out, had that righteousness imputed to the believer for his justification. The foundations of the redemptive construction were thus begun by the divine exposition and promulgation of this essential doctrine; and no little material for the Lord's house was gathered in that period. Glimpses are given of the kind of material collected. Abel was a goodly specimen, not because he was a martyr to the truth; for it is distinctly written that the blood of the lamb, symbolized by his offering, "speaketh better things than the blood of Abel." It was his righteousness by faith which wrought him into the holy fabric and made him a preacher of righteousness, not merely in his day and generation, but to the end of time. This is his epitaph, "By faith Abel offered unto God a more excellent sacrifice than Cain, by which he obtained witness that he was righteous, God testifying of his gifts: and by it he being dead, yet speaketh." So noted was the progress of the work in the days of Enos that it is recorded, "Then began men to call upon the name of the Lord." In another generation we find a man of the highest type of godly character, of whom it is written, "And Enoch walked with God three hundred years; and he was not, for God took him." The gospel of this period, like that subsequently preached by the Carpenter's Son, who did not hesitate to say to the gainsaying, "Behold, your house is left unto you desolate," was not only the accents of tender compassion. The divine apostle said to the incorrigible, "My spirit shall not always strive with man." A specimen of Enoch's preaching against the abominably wicked is preserved, "And Enoch also, the seventh from Adam, prophesied of these saying, Behold the Lord cometh"— the Lord Jesus—"with ten thousands of his saints to execute judgment upon all, and to convince all that are ungodly among them of all their ungodly deeds, which they have ungodly committed, and of all their hard speeches which ungodly sinners have spoken against him,"—the Lord Jesus. To this passage the preserver of it adds an exhortation to the saints to keep themselves in the love of God, "building up yourselves on your most holy faith, and looking for the mercy of our Lord Jesus Christ unto eternal life." In those days a broad line of demarcation was drawn between "the sons of men" and the "sons of God." Some that were called by the latter name lapsed; and their brethren might have said then as it is said now: "They went out from us because they were not of us." And but for the elective line that ran down from Adam to Noah through Seth (who was given in the place of the murdered Abel), as it ran, through Shem, from Noah to Abraham, how could any have been saved? And what shall be said of Noah, the preacher of righteousness, elected from all the myriads of the human family to preserve the seed of man and beast and bird and creeping things from the universal pouring of Divine wrath upon the lamb-despising and Lord-rejecting children of men? God had seen that the wickedness of man was great in the earth, and that every imagination of the thoughts of his heart was only evil continually. And the Lord said, "I will destroy man whom I have created from the face of the earth; both man and beast, and the creeping things and the fowls of the air; for it repenteth me that I have made them." "But Noah" (of whom his father, when naming him, said, "This same shall comfort us concerning our work and toil of our hands, because of the ground which the Lord hath cursed"), "found grace in the eyes of the Lord." Noah found grace: he was saved, as Paul was, by grace through faith and that not of himself—it was the gift of God. Of the rest of the world it was written by the Lord, "And behold I, even I do bring a flood of waters upon the earth, to destroy all flesh wherein is the breath of life from under heaven; and everything that is in the earth shall die. But with thee," said he to Noah, "will I establish my Covenant." What Covenant was this? Not the Covenant with Adam; for that was a Covenant of works, which demanded fidelity equally on the side of each party. But, the Covenant which the Lord calls "my Covenant" is the one made in eternity between the persons of the godhead, and to which Paul refers when, in contrasting it with a legal Covenant, he says, "But, God is one"—the sole dependence of the Covenant of grace.

Fearful were the abominations of these times : " The earth was corrupt before God and the earth was filled with violence. And God looked upon the earth, and behold, it was corrupt; and all flesh had corrupted his way upon the earth." But, was there no mercy in him who was slain as the Lamb of God, to take away the sin of the world? Abounding was his grace, but sin super-abounded. In no period of the redemptive construction was there more extreme exhibition of grace than was made in those days, according to the words of the Apostle Peter : " For Christ also hath suffered for sins, the just for the unjust, that he might bring us unto God, being put to death in the flesh, but quickened by the spirit ; by which also he went and preached unto the spirits in prison, which sometime were disobedient, when once the long suffering of God waited in the days of Noah, while the ark was a preparing, wherein few, that is eight souls were saved by water." This was the limit of even infinite grace ; and the line was passed when his spirit could no longer "strive with men," as it was in later days when it was awfully decreed : " Ephraim is joined to his idols, let him alone." Man was only allowed to do his own will and have his own way. What can he charge against God? But, the decrees of eternal election must be fulfilled, and Noah is commanded to build an ark for saving of his house ; which ark, not less perfect in its construction than the Tabernacle or the Temple, was a fit symbol of the House of God constructing by grace, through the ages, for the salvation of the family of the Most High.   Peter had an eye to this symbolism when he, referring to the Ark, says, " Wherein few, that is eight souls were saved by water.   The like figure where-unto even baptism doth also now save us (not the putting away of the filth of the flesh, but the answer of a good conscience toward God), by the resurrection of Jesus Christ: who is gone into heaven; angels and authorities and powers being made subject unto him."

But, the ark was no more designed to symbolize the salvation of the believing children of God than the flood was designed to symbolize the destruction of the disobedient and disbelieving children of man.   The one was a type of the work of the grace of God; the other, of the work of the wrath of the Lamb.   The wrath that destroyed the world once by water will destroy it again by fire; and the avenging angel is in both cases the despised evangel.   There is no wrath like " the wrath of the Lamb."   The great curse came, and no living thing remained on the earth.   "And Noah alone remained alive and they that were with him in the ark."

It is worthy of note that while the Lord commanded that only two of all other animals should be saved, he ordered that seven of all "clean" animals should be taken into the ark.   Thus was great prominence given to the sacrificial idea, which was the great idea of the true religion of those times, as it has been of all times. No sooner did Noah come out of the ark than he built an altar unto the Lord, and offered upon it of every

6

clean beast and bird that had been saved. Thus the
Lord began the new world by glorifying the great truth
of Christ, and him crucified. And the Covenant of
grace was more formally established with Noah, and
with all the living creatures about him, over which he
was given control as it was given to Adam, and whose
fate was to be the fate of their representing Lord. And
of this Covenant the bow, set in the heavens, was to
be a memorial forever; and that the Covenant might
be never forgotten as a Covenant of grace, the same bow
is seen, in apocalytic vision, to surround the throne of
him who has on his vesture a name written, "King of
kings, and Lord of lords," but who might appropriately
have emblazoned on his diadem: THE CARPENTER'S
SON.

Thus in the antediluvian period were established the
doctrines of elective grace, salvation by the righteousness which is by faith in the divine Lamb of God, and
final destruction by the wrath of the Lamb of all dis-
believers of his name. The world's greatest sin, in all
times, is disbelief. Hence, said the Carpenter's Son, the
Spirit of God shall "reprove the world of sin, because
they believe not in me." The antediluvian doctrines
are the essential principles of the redemptive construction. And of the two most illustrious examples of the
two first principles—both men, by nature and in family, sinners—we have these records: "By faith Enoch
was translated that he should not see death: and was
not found because God had translated him; for before
his translation he had this testimony that he pleased

God. But, without faith it is impossible to please him; for he that cometh to God must believe that he is, and that he is a rewarder of them that diligently seek him. By faith, Noah being warned of God of things not seen as yet, moved with fear, prepared an ark to the saving of his house; by the which he condemned the world, and became heir of the righteousness which is by faith." A further testimony is given of the righteousness of Noah, which was by faith, when the prophet Ezekiel, who was impressing upon his people the certainty of the calamities which should come upon the land if they should "trespass grievously," said twice in quick succession, "Though these three men, Noah, Daniel and Job, were in it, they should deliver but their own souls by their righteousness, saith the Lord God." Yes, the testimony is God's himself: "Though these three men were in it, as I live saith the Lord God, they shall deliver neither sons nor daughters; they only shall be delivered, but the land shall be desolate." And once again Jehovah repeats: Though Noah were in the land! Thus it will be, in the end of our sinful world, the righteousness and faith of no man shall save a single soul—only the righteousness, which is by faith, of the Lord Jesus Christ.

The name of Noah goes down the ages as the builder of the first great symbol of the Kingdom of Heaven, the ark in which are found these prime elements of the House of God: 1. It was of God. 2. It covered the elect, though not without righteousness. 3. It was all of grace. 4. The provisions were abundant, conspicuous among which were those relating to the atoning sacrifice. 5. The salvation was sure and complete. 6. All perished who were not in the ark. 7. It was a work of faith and obedience.—Heb. xi. 7.

The Ark of Noah was one of the pivotal points of human history, representing the building work, for which lived and died the Carpenter's Son.

CHAPTER XII.

ABRAHAM.

And he believed in the Lord; and he counted it to him for righteousness.—Gen. xv. 6.

THE wrath of God washed away the God-defiant sinners of earth by the waters of the flood; but the Divine Mercy did not destroy the nature of sin in the elect by the salvation of the Ark. Even Noah, the righteous, had no sooner landed from the structure symbolic of the great salvation by grace, and renewed his solemn Covenant with the Lord, than he was guilty of gross sin, which caused his curse upon his grandson that lasts until this day. And so rampant in their pride became the descendants of the great preacher of righteousness that they attempted to defy the divine providence by the building of a city, and a tower "whose top may reach unto heaven." The striking record is, that the Lord came down from heaven to see the city and tower, and seeing that the building was not in harmony with his redemptive construction, he confounded the builders and scattered them over the face of the earth. Yet there were some elect among them. The founder of the city—Babel—was a mighty hunter "before the Lord." And because he was this, it passed into a proverb: "Even as Nimrod the mighty hunter before the

85

Lord." Here appeared in post-diluvian man, what had appeared in the antediluvian, that the living material for the Lord's house must be by the election of grace. And thus came prominently in the history of this period Abram, of whom the motto of this chapter is written.

In the call and election of Abram by the Carpenter's Son, he appeared personally to him. In Haran, where he bade Abram "Get thee out of thy country, . . . and I will make of thee a great nation," the Lord *spake* unto Abram. In the plain of Moreh, where the Lord promised: "Unto thy seed will I give this land," it is written, "The Lord appeared unto Abram." After Abram's interview with Melchizedek and the King of Sodom, the record is that "the Lord came unto Abram in a vision," promising that "he that shall come forth of thine own bowels shall be thine heir." But, as the man of God was sitting in his tent door in the plains of Mamre, the Carpenter's Son came to him, as he appeared to Peter and to John when he called them, in the person of a man, whom the Patriarch entertained with a calf "tender and good" from his flock, and with whom he, accompanying him, had a protracted interview with regard to the doom of the cities of the plain. The narrative of their interview concludes: "And the Lord went his way as soon as he had left communing with Abraham; and Abraham returned unto his place." Thus we see that the man of God knew Jesus; he had been with him, and talked and prayed to him, and knew him in that highest and best sense that all the effectually called and elected know him : hence he followed him to a land he knew not of; believed him as to things that he could not see nor understand ; and obeyed him in commands that seemed opposed to nature and to God. This was the faith of the Father of the Faithful that was imputed to him for righteousness, and is the model of evangelical faith given to the ages.

Abraham was not a perfect man. He dealt harshly with Hagar, whose name for Jehovah who came to her relief, "Thou God seest me," seems to be a rebuke to the patriarch. Deliberately he agreed with Sarah to deceive the Pharaoh of Egypt and the Abimelech of Gerar, to his own advantage and to their injury. And both these heathen kings reproved the man of God. But, God did not call him because he was a model man, but in order that he might be made a model for sinners like himself. Hence, in the midst of his sin with the King of Gerar, the Lord commended him—not his sin —to Abimelech, saying : "He is a prophet, and he shall pray for thee, and thou shalt live." The believing world is to follow the Father of the Faithful so far as he followed the Carpenter's Son.

The elements of Abraham's character, generous by nature and ennobled by the grace of God, are given because he is the chief specimen of the living material for the Lord's house presented to all generations by the word of God. His faith was great. But it was no greater than the promises on which it was founded. When he was called to follow the Lord, he was prom-

ised, " In thee shall all families of the earth be blessed."
After his generous separation from Lot, the Lord appeared to him and said, "I will make thy seed as the
dust of the earth : so that if a man can number the dust
of the earth, then shall thy seed also be numbered." In
order to keep before his mind this promise, his name
was changed, the Lord saying, " Neither shall thy name
any more be called Abram, but thy name shall be Abraham; for a father of many nations have I made thee. . . .
And I will establish my covenant between me and thee
and thy seed after thee in their generations, for an everlasting covenant, to be a God unto thee and to thy seed
after thee." This he believed when he had no legal
child, and had no prospect of such a child ; and after
a son and heir was given to him and the Lord commanded him to sacrifice that son—that only son—he
still believed the promise, because he believed in the
Covenant-keeping Jehovah. And as a reward to this
faith and obedience the promise and Covenant of God
was repeated in a still more emphatic manner, this being
the record: "And the Angel of the Lord called unto
Abraham out of heaven the second time, and said, By
myself have I sworn, saith the Lord ; for because thou
hast done this thing, and hast not withheld thy son—
thine only son—that in blessing I will bless thee, and in
multiplying I will multiply thy seed as the stars of
the heaven, and as the sand which is upon the sea-shore ;
and thy seed shall possess the gate of his enemies ; and
in thy seed shall all the nations of the earth be blessed;
because thou hast obeyed my voice." And the faith of

the believer to-day rests upon the identical ground that Abraham's faith rested on. The person that appears in the gospel and in the believer's life is the same person that communed and covenanted with the Patriarch. And the promise to and the Covenant with this man of God is the Covenant of grace presented in the gospel. Paul declares to the Galatians that the salvation the believer gets in Christ is the blessing promised to the seed of Abraham. None of the family of man since Abraham's day are included in the Covenant of grace, according to the divine election, except the children of Abraham; but all who exercise Abraham's faith in the promise of God, *they* are the children of Abraham. "Even as Abraham believed God and it was accounted to him for righteousness. Know ye, therefore, that they which are of faith the same are the children of Abraham. And the scripture, foreseeing that God would justify the heathen through faith, preached before the gospel unto Abraham, saying, In thee shall all nations be blessed. So then they which be of faith are blessed with faithful Abraham. . . . Now to Abraham and his seed were the promises made. He saith not, And to thy seeds, as of many; but as of one, And to thy seed, which is Christ. . . . For ye are all the children of God by faith in Christ Jesus. . . . And if ye be Christ's, then are ye Abraham's seed, and heirs according to the promise."

This faith of Abraham implied a gracious nature, out of which sprang all the graces of the Spirit. The law of supreme love to God and love to our neighbor as to ourself was regarded by this man of God, though he trusted alone for acceptance to the grace of God. Wherever he goes he builds an altar to the Lord and calls on the name of the Lord; and he listens to the Covenant of the Lord lying with his face on the ground. The memorial of this Covenant is observed in all his house, and the piety of the man of God is happily reflected in even the servants of the family. When his servant goes to get a wife for Isaac, he looks to God for success, praying, "O Lord God of my master Abraham, I pray thee send me good speed this day and show kindness unto my master, Abraham." And when his prayer is answered, it is written, "And the man bowed down his head and worshipped the Lord, saying, Blessed be the Lord God of my master Abraham, who hath not left destitute my master of his mercy and his truth." When he reports to Rebekah's brother the prosperity of Isaac's father, he attributes it all to the Lord. "And the Lord hath blessed my master greatly, and he is become great; and he hath given him flocks and herds, and silver and gold, and men-servants and maid-servants, and camels and asses." There is truth in the proverb, Like master, like servant! Abraham's nature was generous and noble to those near and to those far off. To his nephew Lot he gave the choice of the whole land for his flocks and herds, and when he was robbed and led captive by Chedorlaomer and his royal confederates, the Patriarch marshalled his home-forces and rescued his kinsman with much spoil. But of the spoil would he have none, as he would not accept from

Ephron the field and Cave of Machpelah, saying to the King of Sodom, " I have lifted up mine hand unto the Lord, the most high God, the possessor of heaven and earth, that I will not take from a thread to a shoe-latchet, and that I will not take anything that is thine, lest thou shouldest say, I have made Abram rich." And his intercession for Lot, and for the cities of Sodom and Gomorrah, is the finest specimen of intercessory prayer recorded in the word of God. And it is written " God remembered Abraham, and sent Lot out of the midst of the overthrow, when he overthrew the cities in which Lot dwelt." And worthy of note is it that the revelation of the divine purpose with regard to the cities of the plain, and the greater revelation to Sarah that she should be the mother of the saved nations of the earth, were given by the Lord while enjoying the liberal hospitality of the patriarch's tent. The picture of his conduct is beautifully drawn, " And he sat in the tent door in the heat of the day ; and he lifted up his eyes and looked, and lo, three men stood by him ; and when he saw them he ran to meet them from the tent door, and bowed himself toward the ground, and said: My Lord, if now I have found favor in thy sight, pass not away, I pray thee, from thy servant : Let a little water, I pray you, be fetched and wash your feet, and rest yourselves under the tree, and I will fetch a morsel of bread and comfort ye your hearts ; after that ye shall pass on : for therefore are ye come to your servant. And they said, so do, as thou hast said." How different the treatment of this Lord, in the days of the

Carpenter's Son, who had not where to lay his head!
This conduct of the man of God was an index to his
goodly and godly character, and it was at this time
that the Lord said : "Shall I hide from Abraham that
thing which I do, seeing that Abraham shall surely
become a great and mighty nation, and all the nations
of the earth shall be blessed in him ?   For I know him,
that he will command his children and his household
after him, and they shall keep the way of the Lord, to
do justice and judgment; that the Lord may bring upon
Abraham that which he hath spoken of him." Abraham
was not a fatalist; he was no antinomian.   The Lord
knew that the man of God would work out his own
salvation with fear and trembling, though the Lord
had made a covenant of life with him and was working
in him to will and to do of his own good pleasure. And
is it not this generous, hospitable spirit of the Patriarch
which gave shape to the precept of the gospel, " Be
not forgetful to entertain strangers ; for thereby some
have entertained angels unawares."   The Father of the
Faithful seemed an impersonation of gospel graces,
which are thus summarized by Paul :—Faith, Hope,
Charity — these three, but the greatest of these is
Charity.

And how great the honors conferred upon this man
of God ! Melchizedek, the King of Salem and " the
priest of the most high God," meets him with bread and
wine and exclaims : " Blessed be Abram of the most
high God, possessor of heaven and earth, and blessed
be the most high God which hath delivered thine ene-

mies into thine hand!" To Abraham is given a son, who typifies the miraculous birth of the Carpenter's Son, and is offered upon Mount Moriah as a type of the death and resurrection of the lamb of God, that taketh away the sin of the world! The name that the Lord himself takes is "the God of Abraham;" and the final state of heavenly rest is described as in Abraham's bosom.

Great was the honor to Abraham, but greater was his honoring of the Lord. Melchizedek brought him bread and wine; but he made an offering of a tenth to this priest of the most high God and King of Peace, who was the symbol of the regal and eternal priesthood of him who was known in the days of his humiliation as "the Carpenter's Son;" but who stands in the holy of holies of the heavenly Temple, as our great High Priest "after the order of Melchizedek." Isaac was an honor to his father, but he was a living publication of the grand truths which enter the foundations of the house of God, which is to compass the good of heaven and of earth, and an outline of which was erected most clearly before the vision of Abraham when the Lord declared to him, as if the grand structure of human redemption were already completed, "A father of many nations have I made thee." Thus was great progress made in the dawn of the patriarchal period, the very best material being selected, and the whole structure being revealed so sure of success that it is presented as if already complete! Abraham's vision of the certified glory is thus depicted, "He looked for a city which hath foundations whose maker and builder is God."

CHAPTER XIII.

PATRIARCHAL PERIOD.

OTHER PATRIARCHS.

Jacob have I loved, but Esau have I hated.—Rom. ix. 13.

IN the part of this period from Abraham to Moses, some fine material was selected and some very poor. The two extremes, Isaac and Joseph, were beautiful characters, intermediate ones were more or less hateful. One dark spot—his falsehood in Gerar—blurs Isaac's fame; none Joseph's fair name. What shall be said of the lying and crafty Jacob, and the incestuous and brother-stealing Judah? Yet they are the chosen of the Lord, "that the purpose of God, according to election, might stand, not of works, but of him that calleth." And a special design of this period seems the illustration of the absolute arbitrariness of the divine selection. It is distinctly stated that, before the twin-brothers, Esau and Jacob, were born, the latter was chosen above the former. And God's sovereignty in the matter is made more conspicuous by the divine purpose being carried out through the despicable conduct of Jacob's heartless shrewdness to secure his brother's birthright, and his blasphemous falsehood to secure his father's blessing; just as appeared in the decreed crucifixion of the Carpenter's Son, of whom Peter said to his murderers, "Him being delivered by the determinate counsel and foreknowledge of God, ye have taken, and by wicked hands have crucified and slain." And when Paul is discussing the divine sovereignty in the ninth chapter of Romans, he cites this very case of Jacob and Esau to illustrate that the Almighty "hath mercy on whom he will have mercy and whom he will he hardeneth." And how arbitrary the blessing of Ephraim above his older brother Manasseh, which the blinded Jacob had to do in an unnatural manner, and with the displeasure of Joseph, the darling of his bosom and the preserver of the life of his father and family! "So then," says Paul, "it is not of him that willeth, nor of him that runneth, but of God that showeth mercy."

ISAAC.

The splendid faith of Abraham overshadows that of his son's, but the faith of Isaac is worthy not to be overlooked. At an early age this only Son of the Father of the Faithful must have learned that in him was the hope of the ages. The promise to Abraham was, "In Isaac shall thy seed be called." What then must have been his sentiments when bound on the altar in Mount Moriah? What must have been his faith to be offered without a struggle or word? If the language applied by Isaiah to the Lamb of God that taketh away the sin of the world were applied to the typical Isaac the application would be complete, "He is brought as a lamb to the slaughter, and as a sheep before her shearers is dumb so he opened not his mouth." And did the Evangelist Philip make no allusion to

Isaac when from this passage from the prophet "he preached unto the Ethiopian *Jesus?*" The faith of Isaac was probably thus sent through Ethiopia, and has thus been published, by the New Testament, throughout the world. Abraham's faith, in this transaction, was the faith of the priest who offers the lamb; the faith of Isaac, that of the voluntary lamb offered— the lamb of God himself! The language of the author of the Hebrews is equally applicable to the son with the father, "Accounting that God was able to raise him up, even from the dead ; from whence also he received him in a figure." From the time of this offering of himself, Isaac must have been a conscious, living evangel, carrying in himself the most striking publication of the truth as it is in Jesus that had ever been given to man. It is written of the faithful before his day, "These all died in faith, not having received the promises, but having seen them afar off, and were persuaded of them, and embraced them, and confessed that they were strangers and pilgrims on the earth." Isaac too was a stranger and a pilgrim, but the promise was as nigh as his own person—the promise of Christ who, as the Lamb of God, was symbolized in Isaac's personal offering. Immediately after his father "gave up the ghost," the Lord appeared unto Isaac and "blessed him, and Isaac dwelt by the well Lahai-roi." The meaning of this dwelling-place is: "Of the living one who beholdest me." This associates itself with the *Jehovah-jireh* of Mount Moriah, "In the mountain of the Lord it shall be seen." In that mountain *has been* seen the foundations and edifice of the great type of the kingdom of heaven, whose main feature is the Lamb of God, ever beheld in emblem, by the living one, in the typical Isaac. The identical promise to the father is given to the Son, "I will make thy seed to multiply as the stars of heaven, . . . and in thy seed shall all the nations of the earth be blessed." But, that this might be realized by him as it was by his father, not to be according to nature, but by the election of grace, his wife also brings forth as an answer to special intercession. "And Isaac entreated the Lord for his wife, because she was barren: and the Lord was entreated of him, and Rebekah his wife conceived." The Lord Jehovah appeared to him again and again; and he erected altars to him on which were offered sacrifices only less acceptable than his own sacrifice of himself; and he lived long enough to see fully established in his family the mysterious working of God's elective grace. Contrary to his own choice, he bestows the blessing, to be transmitted, upon Jacob, and that, by faith, before his son had seen Rachel or Leah. "God Almighty bless thee," said the aged patriarch, "and make thee fruitful, and multiply thee, that thou mayest be a multitude of people; and give thee the blessing of Abraham, to thee, and to thy seed with thee; that thou mayest inherit the land wherein thou art a stranger, which God gave unto Abraham." The man of God sees the disinherited Esau taking wives of the daughters of Canaan, "which were a grief of mind unto Isaac and Rebekah;" and twenty years after he had bestowed the

7

blessing upon Jacob, he welcomes him back to the land of promise, with wives from the family from which Abraham sprang; with superabundance of the blessings of this world, according to the blessing-prayer of his father, "Therefore God give thee of the dew of heaven, and the fatness of the earth, and plenty of corn and wine;" with tidings that the man Christ Jesus had appeared unto him in person, and changed his name, and given him a name that indicated that he was a prince in the spiritual service of prayer, and a name by which the people of God shall be known in all ages of the world; with the heir apparent to the divine promises already born; and with the whole land for possession undisputed before him, his rival and hating brother, Esau, being reconciled and having emigrated with abundance from the land of promise. The blessing of Abraham upon Isaac had passed fully from Isaac to Jacob, who erected an altar, with the significant name, El-Elohe-Israel, "God, the God of Israel." First, Jehovah, the Lord Jesus, was "the God of Abraham;" then "the God of Abraham and the God of Isaac." Now, he is "the God of Abraham, and Isaac, and Jacob." "And Isaac gave up the ghost and died, and was gathered unto his people, being old and full of days; and his sons, Esau and Jacob, buried him."

JACOB.

Jacob's experience was a bitter and a blessed one. He had no confidence in his children, except the two by his beloved Rachel; and these ten children were a lying, licentious, murderous set, the exaggerations of the early folly and wickedness of their father, who, knowing himself, had no faith in them. They did not deceive him even in the case of their crime against the beloved Joseph; for thirteen years after they thought they had imposed upon the old man's credulity, he said to them: "Me have ye bereaved of Joseph." He felt that he was in constant danger of having his "gray hairs brought down with sorrow to the grave." And, in his dying hours, he surprised them by prophecies of their future derived from his treasured knowledge of the past, and the inspiration of God. His own deception of his aged father Isaac, and his ill-treatment of his brother Esau, all by the craft of his mother, Rebekah, which he seems to have inherited, came back upon him in his mother's family in Padan-aram, and in the terror with which his brother subsequently inspired him. But Jacob was a man of decided parts, and neither Laban nor Esau got ahead of him—though it hurt him badly, perhaps, that he had to buy off Esau at so high a price!

But Jacob was the elect of God. The great Architect of all took him, as he took the cursing Peter and the persecuting Saul, to show his power in changing him into material meet for the heavenly work. Jacob communed "face to face" with the Carpenter's Son, which he commemorated by the name he gave to the place where he wrestled with the nameless "man" for blessing—the name "Peniel." But, twenty years before this he had seen in vision a ladder reaching from earth to heaven, on which angels were ascending and descending. "And, behold, the Lord stood above it and said, I am the Lord God of Abraham thy father, and the God of Isaac; the land whereon thou liest to thee will I give it, and to thy seed; and thy seed shall be as the dust of the earth; and thou shalt spread abroad to the west, and to the east, and to the north, and to the south; and in thee and in thy seed shall all the families of the earth be blessed." Here was the same old glorious promise to Abraham, which had been bestowed by Isaac, coming upon the elected Jacob from the lips of Jehovah himself. So awfully sacred and blessed was this place that he erected a pillar, in commemoration, and poured oil upon it, calling it Bethel, for said he, "This is none other but the house of God, and this the gate of heaven!" And Jacob vowed a vow unto the Lord, and he was a new man. While in Padan-aram, the Lord appeared in person to him, calling himself the "God of Bethel where thou anointedst the pillar, and vowed a vow unto me," and his promised blessing never forsook the patriarch, who prospered ever by the hand of the Lord, as is the distinct record of the Spirit, and as was ever most humbly acknowledged by himself. Returning to the land of promise, and to his father Isaac, and dreading encounter with the injured Esau, he makes this confession and appeal: "Oh, God of my father Abraham, and God of my father Isaac, the Lord that said unto me: Return unto thy country and to thy kindred, and I will deal well with thee; I am not worthy of the least of all the mercies and of all the truth, which thou hast showed unto thy servant; for with my staff I passed over this Jordan, and now I am become two bands. Deliver me, I pray thee, from the hand of my brother, from the hand of Esau; for I fear him, lest he will come and smite me, and the mother with the children. And thou saidest, I will surely do thee good, and make thy seed as the sand of the sea, which cannot be numbered for multitude." This is the humble cry of a believing man of God. And he shows his faith by his works. He goes to Bethel—"the house of God;" he strips from his family all the idols and signs of paganism and buries them out of sight; and thus he " calls upon the name of the Lord." And not only is he delivered from Esau, by the hand of the Lord directing Jacob's own practical wisdom, but "the terror of God was upon the cities that were round about them, and they did not pursue after the sons of Jacob." And evermore was the Lord with him, protecting, guiding, sanctifying and comforting. His greatest sorrow—the loss of Joseph—was more than compensated by finding him again, in such a position of usefulness and honor, and heaping coals upon his unnatural brothers by the preservation of their lives and the most unmeasured kindness to the whole family. He was honored by the friendship of the Pharaoh of Egypt, to whose inquiry of the venerable man of God, "How old art thou?" he beautifully and pathetically replied, " The days of the years of my pilgrimage are one hundred and thirty years: few and evil have the days of the years of my life been, and have not attained unto the days of the years of the life of my fathers in the days of their pilgrimage.

And Jacob blessed Pharaoh, and went out from before Pharaoh." He had the inspired forecast to see the destiny of all his household; and the spiritual honesty to tell the whole truth. And when he "gathered up his feet in his bed, and yielded up the ghost, and was gathered to his people," he was honored by perhaps the grandest international funeral procession that ever followed mortal remains. "And Joseph went up to bury his father; and with him went up all the servants of Pharaoh, the elders of his house, and all the elders of the land of Egypt. And all the house of Joseph, and his brethren, and his father's house; . . . and there went up with him both chariots and horsemen; and it was a very great company." And they mourned with "a very sore lamentation" for seven days. So that when the inhabitants of the land, the Canaanites, saw it, they said: "This is a grievous mourning to the Egyptians." Thus was fulfilled in him personally what his father had prayed in his blessing: "Let people serve thee and nations bow down to thee. . . . Cursed be every one that curseth thee, and blessed be he that blesseth thee;" and more especially what the Lord had said unto him, "And behold I am with thee, and will keep thee in all places whither thou goest, and will bring thee again into this land; for I will not leave thee, until I have done that of which I have spoken to thee of. . . . I will go down with thee unto Egypt; and I will also surely bring thee up again; and Joseph shall put his hands upon thine eyes." And they buried him in the cave of the field of Machpelah, which Abraham bought with the field for a possession of a burying-place of Ephron, the Hittite, before Mamre."

Israel's house that went into Egypt were " seventy souls."   They had increased when Moses brought them out, perhaps twenty thousand-fold.   How many of these, and of those that died in Egypt and in Canaan, the Carpenter's Son selected, for the permanent house of the Lord, there is no record of save in the Lamb's book of life !

CHAPTER XIV.

OTHER PATRIARCHS.

JUDAH.

The sceptre shall not depart from Judah . . . until Shiloh come.—
Gen. xlix. 10.

JUDAH was the fourth son of Jacob by his first wife, the "tender-eyed" Leah. His name means praise. He married the daughter of Shuah, and two of his sons —"wicked in the sight of the Lord"—died in Canaan. The sons that went into Egypt were Shelah, Pharez and Zarah. Pharez's sons were Hezron and Hamul. In the genealogy of the Carpenter's Son—" the son of Abraham "—we read: " Abraham begat Isaac; and Isaac begat Jacob; and Jacob begat Judas and his brethren; and Judas begat Pharez and Zarah of Thamar; and Pharez begat Ezrom, *etc.*" Thus was the son of the Virgin Mary derived directly, according to human descent from Judah; and he is called, indeed, "the lion of the tribe of Judah."

Judah was chief among his brethren, but in the flesh he, like his sons Er and Onan, was wicked in the sight of the Lord. When he declared that Tamar, his daughter-in-law, the mother of his twin boys Pharez and Zarah, should be burnt, he was pronouncing the capital sentence due to his own crime. It was he also that sold Joseph to the Midianite merchantmen, going into Egypt. But,

104

the divine call of Judah is only another illustration of
the elective grace of God, and of the power of the Lord
unto the vilest of the children of man. And meet was
it that Judah, who had sold his brother into Egypt,
should be most prominent in the agonizing interviews
with his aged father about Benjamin's going into Egypt;
and with the exalted governor of the house of Pharaoh
who had ordered it. When the sons of Jacob returned
from Egypt with the corn they had bought, to save from
starvation their father's house in Canaan, without Simeon
and with the demand that Benjamin should go back with
them, as the condition prescribed for getting any more
corn, the heart of the old man was torn in grief. He
more than intimated that they had killed their brothers,
crying, "Me have ye bereaved of my children; Joseph
is not, and Simeon is not, and ye will take Benjamin
away; all these things are against me." Reuben, his
first-born, had protested, "Slay my two sons, if I bring
him not to thee;" but the old man said, "My son shall
not go down with you, . . . ye bring down my gray
hairs with sorrow to the grave." But Judah, the strong-
est of the brethren, throws himself into the painful col-
loquy, and with smitings of conscience as he witnesses
his father's anguish about Joseph, and his darling last-
born, he, with more ingenuity than Reuben, rather demands, "Send the lad with me, and we will arise and
go; that we may live and not die, both we, and those,
and also our little ones. I will be surety for him; of
my hand shalt thou require him; if I bring him not
unto thee, and set him before thee, then let me bear the

blame forever." The old man, yielding, said: "God Almighty give you mercy before the man, that he may send away your other brother, and Benjamin. If I be bereaved, I am bereaved." And did not God Almighty have mercy on Judah's soul also? And how terribly is his heart wrung now, when, after they get the corn and are returning with it and Benjamin, they are arrested because of the silver cup found in Benjamin's sack! It is written, "And Judah and his brethren came to Joseph's house; and they fell before him on the ground. And Judah said, What shall we say unto my lord?— What shall we speak? or how shall we clear ourselves? God hath found out the iniquity of thy servants; behold we are my lord's servants, both we, and he also with whom the cup is found." What a revelation this speech to the lord of Pharaoh's house of the aroused conscience of Judah as well as of the agony of his heart. But, the steel must be driven deeper into his soul by the spiritual sagacity of the man and by the grace of God. Judah's cup was full when the lord said, "God forbid that I should do so : but the man in whose hand the cup is found, he shall be my servant: and as for you, get you up in peace unto your father." Think of the fearfully mocking words, *in peace unto your father!* This was too much for human nature to endure. The man that "spake as never man spake" was no doubt by the side of the elected Judah from whom he himself in the flesh was to spring, and the son of Jacob and the brother of Benjamin gave utterance to the most beautiful and touching address of which there is record on any page sacred or profane. It is worthy to be studied as a perfect model of natural, and gracious pathos, nothing less than the inspiration of the Carpenter's Son himself, who is touched by a feeling of our infirmities and was himself a man of sorrows and acquainted with grief. "Then Judah came near unto him, and said, Oh my lord, let thy servant, I pray thee, speak a word in my lord's ears, and let not thine anger burn against thy servant; for thou art even as Pharaoh. My lord asked his servants, saying, Have ye a father or a brother? And we said unto thy lord, We have a father, an old man, and a child of his old age, a little one; and his brother is dead and he alone is left of his mother, and his father loveth him. And thou saidst unto thy servants, Bring him down unto me, that I may set mine eyes upon him. And we said unto my lord, The lad cannot leave his father; for if he should leave his father, his father would die. And thou saidst unto thy servants, Except your youngest brother come down with you, ye shall see my face no more. And it came to pass when we came up unto thy servant my father, we told him the words of my lord. And our father said, Go again and bring us a little food. And we said, We cannot go down: if our youngest brother be with us, then will we go down: for we may not see the man's face, except our youngest brother be with us. And thy servant my father said unto us, Ye know that my wife bare me two sons: And the one went out from me and I said, Surely he is torn in pieces; and I saw him not since: And if ye take this also from me, and mischief befall him, ye shall

bring down my gray hairs with sorrow to the grave.
Now, therefore, when I come to thy servant my father,
and the lad is not with us ; seeing that his life is bound
up in the lad's life; it shall come to pass, when he seeth
that the lad is not with us, that he will die : and thy
servants shall bring down the gray hairs of thy servant
our father with sorrow to the grave.   For thy servant
became surety for the lad unto my father, saying, If
I bring him not unto thee, then shall I bear the blame
to my father forever.   Now, therefore, I pray thee, let
thy servant abide instead of the lad, a bondman to my
lord ; and let the lad go up with his brethren.   For
how shall I go up to my father, and the lad be not with
me ? lest peradventure I see the evil that shall come
upon my father."

This broke Joseph's heart.   He could stand it no
longer.   He wept aloud, so that the Egyptians and the
house of Pharaoh heard, saying: "I am Joseph your
brother, whom ye sold into Egypt.   Now, therefore, be
no more grieved nor angry with yourselves that ye sold
me hither ; for God did send me before you to preserve
life.   .   .   .   And he fell upon his brother Benjamin's
neck, and wept ; and Benjamin wept upon his neck.
Moreover, he kissed his brethren, and wept upon them ;
and after that his brethren talked with him."

This is what the eloquent speech of Judah did ; and
more did it, by the grace of God, it brought up to Egypt
the aged patriarch, who, when dying, pronounced the
blessing upon Judah thus : "Judah thou art he whom
thy brothers shall praise ; thy hand shall be in the neck

of thy enemies; thy father's children shall bow down before thee. Judah is a lion's whelp: from the prey, my son, thou art gone up: he stooped down, he crouched as a lion, and as an old lion; who shall rouse him up? The Sceptre shall not depart from Judah, nor a lawgiver from between his feet, until Shiloh come; and unto him shall the gathering of the people be. Binding his foal unto the vine, and his ass's colt unto the choice vine; he washed his garments in wine, and his clothes in the blood of grapes; his eyes shall be red with wine and his teeth white with milk."

And the Lord was ever with the house of Judah. In the numbering in the wilderness his family numbered "three-score and sixteen thousand and five hundred." When the elders of the people wished to bless the marriage of Boaz and Ruth they said to Boaz, a progenitor of the family of the Carpenter's Son, "Let thy house be like the house of Pharez, whom Tamar bare unto Judah of the seed which the Lord shall give thee of this young woman."

More celebrated than all the other tribes was the tribe of Judah, and more famous than all other lands was the land of Judah. The name of Judah is mentioned in the word of God not less than eight hundred and twenty-three times. In fact, most of the recorded dealings of God with the world's history is in connection with the tribe and the land of Judah, where were Jerusalem, and the Temple, and Bethlehem of which it is written: "And thou Bethlehem, in the land of Judah, art not the least among the princes of Judah; for out of thee shall come a Governor that shall rule my people Israel."

JOSEPH.

Israel loved Joseph more than all his children.—Gen. **xxx**vii. 3.

Joseph was the most beautiful character of sacred history, the son of Joseph of Nazareth alone excepted. There seemed no need in his biography to make special mention of the Lord's presence with him ; for his whole life was an illustration of his walk with God. He was distinguished among his brethren not merely by his "coat of many colors," but by a character superior to theirs in every respect. He loved God and abhorred evil. Hence the Lord preserved the innocence of his youth, gave him visions of his future greatness, and overruled the envy and hatred of his brothers to his great glory and to their own salvation. In Egypt, the God of Abraham and Isaac and Jacob was manifestly with him, giving him firmness to resist temptation, wisdom to interpret royal dreams, and statesmanship to manage the affairs of a great nation in a fearful emergency, with the most eminent prudence, benevolence and success. The name of God was glorified in this impersonation of divine goodness and graciousness. His dealing with the matter of his brethren and the whole family is beyond praise. His honoring of his father and his forgiveness of his brethren, and his recognition of the divine hand in the whole transaction, while he preserves the greatest fidelity to his office and his king, are thoroughly Christian, and bespeak the Carpenter's Son by his side, his counselor and his friend. And now the highest of honors—higher than the glory of

Egypt—is put upon him by the birthright of Jacob being bestowed upon him. Judah, according to the election, received the blessing to be transmitted, but the birthright is given to Joseph and his sons. The official chronicle (1 Chron. v. 1, 2) is, "Reuben was the first-born of Israel; but, forasmuch as he defiled his father's bed, the birthright was given unto the sons of Joseph, the son of Israel; and the genealogy is not to be reckoned after the birthright. For Judah prevailed above his brethren, and of him came the chief ruler; but, the birthright was Joseph's." Hence the grand blessing of the dying patriarch upon his son, and his son's sons: "Joseph is a fruitful bough, even a fruitful bough by a well; whose branches run over the wall: The archers have sorely grieved him, and shot at him, and hated him: But his bow abode in strength, and the arms of his hands were made strong by the hands of the Mighty God of Jacob (from whence is the shepherd, the stone of Israel); Even by the God of thy father, who shall keep thee; and by the Almighty, who shall bless thee with blessings of heaven above, blessings of the deep that lieth under, blessings of the beasts and of the womb: The blessings of thy father have prevailed above the blessings of my progenitors unto the utmost bound of the everlasting hills: they shall be as the head of Jacob, and on the crown of the head of him that was separate from his brethren. . . . And he blessed the sons of Joseph and said, God, before whom my fathers Abraham and Isaac did walk, the God that fed me all my life long unto this day, the Angel which redeemed me from all evil, bless the lads; and let my name be named on them, and the name of my fathers Abraham and Isaac; and let them grow into a multitude in the midst of the earth. . . . And he blessed them that day saying, In thee shall Israel bless, saying, God make thee as Ephraim and as Manasseh: and he set Ephraim before Manasseh."

But the end comes even to a life so beautiful as Joseph's. "And Joseph said unto his brethren, I die: and God will surely visit you, and bring you out of this land unto the land which he sware to Abraham, to Isaac and to Jacob. And Joseph took an oath of the children of Israel, saying, God will surely visit you, and ye shall carry up my bones from hence. So Joseph died, being a hundred and ten years old: and they embalmed him, and he was put in a coffin in Egypt."

It was said that Jacob's funeral procession was the greatest the world ever saw. But, on reflection, was not Joseph's greater? When Moses led out the six hundred thousand men of war, besides women and children, from Egypt to the promised land, it is written: "And Moses took the bones of Joseph with him; for he had straitly sworn the children of Israel, saying, God will surely visit you; and ye shall carry up my bones away hence with you." And thus was carried across the Red Sea the remains of the man who brought a family into Egypt that it might become a great nation, who now bear him back to the sepulchre of his fathers!

And when Moses came to his end, his blessing upon Joseph was above the blessing of all the other tribes:

"And of Joseph he said, Blessed of the Lord be his land, for the precious things of heaven, for the dew, and for the deep that coucheth beneath, and for the precious fruit brought forth by the sun, and for the precious things put forth by the moon, and for the chief things of the ancient mountains, and for the precious things of the lasting hills, and for the precious things of the earth and the fulness thereof, and for the good will of him that dwelt in the bush : let the blessing come upon the head of Joseph, and upon the top of the head of him that was separate from his brethren. His glory is like the firstling of his bullock, and his horns are like the horns of unicorns ; with them he shall push the people together to the ends of the earth : and they are the ten thousands of Ephraim, and they are the thousands of Manasseh."

And even David, when he would make the most powerful appeal to the Almighty, calls upon him as the God of Joseph, and of his sons Ephraim and Manasseh, and of his brother Benjamin, saying, "Give ear, O Shepherd of Israel, thou that leadest Joseph like a flock ; thou that dwellest between the cherubim, shine forth, Before Ephraim and Benjamin and Manasseh, stir up thy strength, and come and save us."

From these samples of the patriarchal periods, some estimate may be made of the nature and quantity of the material collected for the Lord's house, and the progress of the construction, by the grace and presence of the great architect of all, the τέκτων of Nazareth, who was called the Carpenter's Son. And of the divine care of

8

the Lord's house we get a striking intimation in the fact that from the man and woman called out of Ur of the Chaldees, to start the house of the Lord, there arises a people now perhaps not less than two millions.

CHAPTER XV.

MOSAIC PERIOD.

For the law was given by Moses; but grace and truth came by Jesus Christ.—John i. 17.

THIS period may be represented by three facts: The Passover, the giving of the Law, and the erection of the Tabernacle; which facts, as well as the settlement in Canaan, and the Temple and City of Jerusalem, suggest and imply the elements of organization and congregation for the service of God, which were not known in the Patriarchal period; and which are, in the period before us, a foreshadowing of more perfect organization and congregation of God's people, which lie at the basis of their usefulness, and are the type of their future and eternal state of worship and glory.

THE PASSOVER.

For even Christ our passover is sacrificed for us.—1 Cor. v. 7.

This was a means to an end. God remembered his covenant with Abraham and Isaac and Jacob, and after "the children of Israel" had been four hundred and thirty years in Egypt, and had grown to a multitude so great that it is said "the land was filled with them," he resolved to settle them in the land promised and "flowing with milk and honey." To accomplish this pur-

115

pose three things must be accomplished : The Hebrews themselves must desire to depart ; the hand of Pharaoh must be controlled ; and Israel must revive their faith in the God of their fathers.   The excessive oppression of their task-masters, by the order of Pharaoh providentially brought about, accomplished the first necessity ; for "the Egyptians made their lives bitter with hard bondage."   The last necessity was achieved by the Lord appearing personally to Moses, as the Lord Jehovah, whose name is " I am that I am," and giving him the power to perform wonderful miracles which none others could perform ; so that this man not only became great in the eyes of the Egyptians, but the children of Israel believed in him and in the God who did by him these mighty works.   With regard to Pharaoh, he was a fit subject for ruin.   But God used him awhile to exhibit his glory to his people and to the Egyptians ; and by the supreme method of spreading death through the land, the Lord relaxed the grasp of the hardened tyrant, and he sent away the people ; over whom the Angel of Death had passed because the posts of their doors were besprinkled with the blood of a lamb.   This salvation was the means for giving the highest glory to the Covenant-keeping God, and was the pledge of every other needed good.   The Lord God, who delivers them from death and bondage in Egypt, will, despite their fears, destroy Pharaoh who pursues them ; and Amalek, who, with Og and Sihon, would impede their way.   He will give them, notwithstanding their murmurs, water to drink and bread to eat.   He will organize their mass by the wise suggestion of Jethro in the wilderness. And he, even he, the Jehovah Jesus, will attend them all the way, a pillar of cloud by day, and a pillar of fire by night. The feast of the Passover was, therefore, to be a perpetual ordinance. This would bring the people together in congregational worship of the Lord; this would commemorate a salvation which implies all other blessings of the Lord, and which was worthy to be commemorated by the Sabbath, restored now to honor not only the God of nature, but the God of grace; and this feast was the adumbration of another ordinance which should celebrate a greater salvation, involving all good for time and for eternity, by the blood of the Lamb of God, of whom it is written: "For even Christ our passover is sacrificed for us." And all this matter of Moses and the deliverance of his people had, even in their own eyes, a broader view than merely a chapter of human history, the record being, " By faith, Moses, when he was come to years, refused to be called the Son of Pharaoh's daughter, choosing rather to suffer affliction with the people of God than to enjoy the pleasures of sin for a season ; esteeming the reproach of Christ greater riches than the treasures of Egypt : for he had respect to the recompense of reward. By faith he forsook Egypt, not fearing the wrath of the King ; for he endured, as seeing him who is invisible," with whom he had talked face to face, as the " I am that I am " of this period, and the Carpenter's Son of a period to come. And do not the song of Moses and the timbrel and dance of Miriam, on the eastern bank of the

Red Sea, suggest the joy and praises that should fill the lives of God's people saved, by the blood of the Lamb, with " the great salvation " ?

THE LAW.

What the law could not do in that it was weak through the flesh.—
Rom, viii. 3.

Under the most solemn and awful circumstances, the Lord God gave on Sinai to his people, through Moses, the law which was to replace the obliterated law written on the human heart, and which was subsequently summed up, by the divine giver himself, in supreme love to God and love to neighbor as to self. In addition to the Decalogue, the ten commandments, which lie at the foundation of all other laws acceptable in the sight of God, were given many statutes, for the social, political and religious government of the Theocracy that the Lord was now establishing on earth. And these statutes were not to have application alone to this people. Many of them commend themselves so fully to human reason that a distinguished statesman has remarked that, wherever the laws of men do not accord with these laws, the disposition of the human heart is to follow the statutes of the Almighty rather than the commandments of man's government. This is specially true with regard to laws regulating, or not regulating, social relations. The statutes with regard to religious concerns look commonly to the holiness of the worshipper, whether an official or unofficial—either positive holiness, by the imitation of

divine goodness which is ever making offerings ; or neg-
ative holiness, in purging conscience and heart and life
by the blood of atoning sacrifice. The Priest—the
people's guide—was to have engraven on his forehead :
HOLINESS TO THE LORD. The whole system was a
perfect one, unlike any other that had appeared among
men, and was a distinguishing mark that made the
children of Israel more than ever abhorred by the nations,
and the nations despised by them. Moses protested
before Pharaoh that Israel must go into the wilderness
to worship, for their sacrifices were " abominations to the
Egyptians," who would " stone them." No code could
keep the mind more constantly on the great object of
worship and none could so perfectly develop the moral
nature of man. In fact, no light from above has to this
day improved upon the moral code given by God to
Moses as a standard and regulation for human conduct.
This is the law of holy conduct to-day, as much as it
was in the days of the holy men of old. Paul and
Peter and John were guided by it, as were Moses and
Samuel and Daniel and Nehemiah and all the other
illustrious examples of faith and holiness of the past.
It was declared, when the law was given, that it was to
make Israel a holy nation of royal priests, from which a
Christian apostle borrows the definition of the followers
of the Carpenter's Son, as "a chosen generation, a royal
priesthood, a holy nation." The Carpenter's Son himself said " the law is holy, just and good ;" and David
sings, "The law of the Lord is perfect, converting the
soul: the testimony of the Lord is sure, making wise the

simple. . . . Moreover, by them is thy servant warned, and in keeping of them there is great reward." There could be no higher human perfection than by perfect obedience to this law of God. It is not strange, therefore, that the Hebrews ever held their law in the highest estimation and contended for it with the greatest zeal, whenever it seemed to be assailed. In the days of the Carpenter's Son on earth, this defence appeared a craze, which blinded them even to the miraculous testimony that they were warring against the author and the finisher of the law himself. Any seeming assault upon this divine code was to them *prima facie* evidence either of insanity or of diabolism, which they thought it was duty to God to cast out or destroy.

But, the very day the law was given, Israel proved themselves unequal to its observance by the manufacture of a false god, by the hand of their highest religious official, in contravention of the two first laws of that moral code. This shocking demonstration of human inability to keep God's law threw Moses himself into momentary despair, made him slay three thousand of the idolaters on the spot, and wish to blot himself out as an atonement for the sin. And he positively refused to go forward with the people, without a new guarantee of the Divine presence—the presence of the Covenant-keeping Jehovah, who would fulfill his promises to Abraham and Isaac and Jacob, because he had promised, and not on the ground that their children had kept the exalted and perfect law that he had given amid the thunders and lightnings of Sinai.

And here let it be remarked that the hope of Moses, and Samuel, and Daniel, and Nehemiah, and all the rest of the worthies and godly under the Mosaic system was the identical hope of Abraham and Isaac and Jacob. These three patriarchs were fully conscious of being vile sinners under the law of nature written in their hearts, of which this law of Moses was only a revised transcript. But, they hoped in the Covenant of Grace, as expressed in the promises of Jehovah. The law was to the pious under it the standard of holiness after which they strived; but it was, in no wise, held the ground of their acceptance with God. In fact, the very perfection of the law gave them the greater consciousness of imperfection, drove them more earnestly to the blood of the atoning lamb, and made them cling more tenaciously to the Covenant-keeping Jehovah, as their "shield and exceeding great joy."

Indeed, so exacting was the law, in every department of the theocratic government, and so terrible were the executions of its penalties, all through the legal ages, without regard to name or position—whether the transgressor was peasant, priest, prophet or king, whether man, woman or child—of which we have so many fearful instances in the wilderness and in Canaan, that it might appear that one object of this formal promulgation and of these terrible executions of the law was to drive man, Jew and Gentile, to despair of himself for salvation, and to force him upon the Covenant-keeping God of Abraham and Isaac and Jacob.

When the Carpenter's Son, who had given that law

on Sinai, came to revive more clearly the original ground of human hope, and to show how alone that perfect law could be fulfilled, the Jew, enraged at the implication against his personal righteousness and his prerogatives as the lineal descendant from Abraham, assailed the Son of man as a blasphemer against his law and holy religion, and could be satisfied with nothing short of his blood, while the giver and expounder of the law charged them openly as arrant hypocrites, and the children of the devil himself. And much of the work of the apostolical expounders of the truth was to encounter and overthrow these false notions of the Jew that he had the promise of Abraham by descent and by the fulfillment of the law of God. The first error Paul completely overthrows by showing from Scripture that in the personal family of Abraham himself one son was rejected, while the other was made the heir of the promise; and the claim that the law was the ground of salvation to the Gentile, or to any, he also shows was contrary to the first principles of even human justice. For, says he, "the Covenant which was confirmed before of Christ, the law which was 430 years after cannot disannul that it should make the promise of none effect." Elsewhere he intimates that the law was given "that the offence might abound"—might abound before human consciousness in order to force unto Christ. And he plainly says, "The law was added because of transgression, till the seed should come to whom the promise was made. . . . Wherefore the law was our schoolmaster to bring us to Christ, that we might be justified by faith." As to salvation, the language of the law is, "Cursed is every one that continueth not in all things that are written in the law to do them." Then how can the soul depend on the law for salvation? But, "Christ hath redeemed us from the law, being made a curse for us," and thus he becomes "the end of the law for righteousness to every one that believeth." Hence he affirmed that he came not "to destroy the law but to fulfill." When he gave the law to Moses, talking to him "face to face as a man talketh to his friend," he knew that he alone could fulfill that code, which he proposed to do, as man's substitute, in order to meet the condition of the Covenant of Grace, made in the eternal Council of God, whereon the promise of salvation is made, "without money and without price," as preached by the prophet Isaiah.

A prominent feature of this legal system was the requirement for many and regular "convocations" of the people for worship. In earlier days God's people were known as individuals or families: now they are to appear in great congregations. This was marked progress in the Lord's house, which is not only to be regulated by fixed and known law, but to be presented to men and angels as the frequently congregating Family of God.

TABERNACLE.

Moses was admonished of God when he was about to make the tabernacle: for see, saith he, that thou make all things according to the pattern showed thee in the mountain.—Heb. viii. 5.

The tabernacle was a model—rather a sketch, of the model—of God's house which was to be subsequently erected in the metropolitan city of the children of Israel. And worthy of attention are some of the objects, the elements, the furniture and the offices of this etching of the Lord's house; and also its application to the present House of God.

I. *Objects.*

1. The first object of the tabernacle was to make a place for the regular manifestation of the God of Israel. He had appeared in the bush to Moses; on the top of a ladder to Jacob; in the Mount of the Lord to Isaac; on the plains of Mamre to Abraham. But, now, he is to have for the eyes of Israel a local habitation and a name.—Ex. xxix. 45. The human heart demands some visible representation of the Most High. If God does not give it, man will make it. Hence the idolatries of the world.

2. Another object was for the localization of the religious thoughts and sentiments of the people. There is no association more powerful than that connected with locality. Hence the power of home and school and country. Thus the Lord would concentrate and intensify the religious elements of his people for their greater edification and utility.

3. Again, thus could they be better instructed in their relations to each other, and as a family whose head was the Lord. There might be secret communications to the individual soul, which is very important; but there is much that Israel is to know in common; and the Tabernacle and its surroundings (Ex. 35) afforded the best conditions for its reception.

4. The Tabernacle furnished a rallying point on every emergency. Here the people could repair, hear the voice of the Lord, look into the faces of each other, touch each other's elbows, and be thus better prepared for any special occasion that might come upon them.

5. The reason of this construction being a tabernacle or tent is obvious. They were travelers—"pilgrims and strangers;" and they had to carry with them the house of the Lord. This is suggestive of the great truth that, whatever be our pursuit, whatever our occupation, whatever our locality, whatever our emergency, we may still "dwell in the house of the Lord."

II. *Elements.*

1. The most prominent element was that the Tabernacle was divinely constructed. The Lord did not give merely the order for the erection of this house; he gave a pattern of it in every particular. Not only did he determine the kind of material of every sort, but the quality and shape and color and arrangement. It was the Lord's work in every detail and in the perfect whole.

2. The workmen employed were inspired for their work. It is said, not only that God gave them the spirit of wisdom and understanding to do the work, but that they were possessed of "the spirit of God." They were inspired by God's Spirit, as were the penmen of God's word.

3. Another element was that the material for the construction was the contribution of willing hearts.

Not only were "the wise-hearted" called upon, but "the willing-minded." And only the material of such went into the structure. It is well to note here that it is a *wise* thing to build the house of the Lord; and that these builders were so liberally-minded that they had to be checked in their contributions; for the offerings they made were "too much."

4. And this construction went up amid the adverse circumstances of a life in the wilderness, traveling, and surrounded by enemies, as if to suggest that God's work, with his presence, does not depend on what seem, in the eyes of men, favorable circumstances. "Not by might, nor power, but by my Spirit, saith the Lord."

III. *Furniture and Offices.*

1. There was furniture for purification, for offerings, for sacrifices, for instruction, for the testimony of the divine presence in the past, and for his present manifestation.

2. There were offices for the stated and proper observances of the Lord's house, and places for all classes of worshippers. Especially were there arrangements for the great atonement-sacrifice, which the High Priest was to make for the sins of the people, without which there could be no divine manifestation.

3. Finally, there was the awful symbol of the Lord God before the eyes of the people, which appeared as the crowning of the completed work, and never forsook the children of Israel in their journey. The record is, "So Moses finished the work. Then a cloud covered

the tent of the congregation, and the glory of the Lord filled the tabernacle. And Moses was not able to enter into the tent of the congregation, because the cloud abode thereon, and the glory of the Lord filled the tabernacle. . . . And the cloud of the Lord was upon the tabernacle by day, and fire was upon it by night, in the sight of all the house of Israel, throughout all their journeys."

IV. *Application of Tabernacle.*

The Tabernacle was an imposing symbol. It originated in Mount Sinai blazing, like a furnace, with the presence of the Lord God. It was twin born with the Law and the Judgments of Jehovah. These latter were instituted for the foundation of character, individual and associated, with reference to duty to God and to man. They were didactic—to be learned by the mind and by the heart. The tabernacle was a picture of the character as it should be, embodying to the eye all of the elements of reformed humanity and of the kingdom of heaven, not only so far as they had been, but as they should be developed in the history of the world and the grace of God to his chosen people. In the material and construction and furniture and appointments of the Tabernacle, as has been said, there were plainly set forth in figure, the elements of character, individual and associated, which it was the will of God to upbuild among men : 1. Elected. 2. God ordained. 3. Costly. 4. Harmonious. 5. Beautiful. 6. Glorious. 7. By the needed altar. 8. With a consecrated Priesthood.

9. All under the Divine presence, on a Mercy Seat, over the ark of the testimony of his holiness, grace, and power; and flanked by emblems of him as the bread of life and the light of the world.

But some of the features of this picture of the character of the kingdom of heaven and its subjects should be noticed more in detail. See: 1. The costliness of the tabernacle, as given in the 38th chapter of Exodus, was great; and how costly the kingdom of heaven erected by offering more precious than silver and gold. Might not each ask, "What the price of my soul? What should I not give to complete God's house on earth, in heaven?"

2. The material most freely offered by the "wise-hearted" and "willing-minded," so that the offerings had to be restrained; thus the kingdom must be up-builded by minds and hearts made free and loving by the regenerating power of the Holy Spirit.

3. The directors of this building were wise-hearted men, in whom "the Lord had put the spirit of wisdom and understanding." Thus should it be in the edification of the house of the Lord—the leaders must be the called and the sanctified of the Lord. The extreme consecration of the High Priest by washing, anointing, clothing with "holy garments," and by publication from the engraven gold on his person of "Holiness to the Lord," typified the perfect High Priest who enters into the Holy of Holies in heaven; and he says to his ministers and to the "royal priesthood," BE YE HOLY AS I AM HOLY.

4. And what exactness in repeating every part of the work done on and in the Tabernacle to show that it was exactly according to the pattern previously detailed as " the pattern given in the Mount." This repetition is intensely interesting. It gives an awfulness to the matter of erecting the house of the Lord. Should the real house be less carefully erected than the model? How should the builders cry: " Lord, what wouldest thou have us to do?" And, if they expect God's glory to fill the house and abide upon it, should it not be said of it, as it is written of the Tabernacle: " the children of Israel did according to all that the Lord commanded Moses. . . . And Moses did look upon all the work, and behold, they had done it as the Lord had commanded, even so had they done it: and Moses blessed them."

5. The Tabernacle was a three-fold covering for the Divine presence with God's people ; so must he not be enshrined in the three-fold nature of his children ?

6. As to the work of that presence, was it not represented by the contents of the Ark of the Covenant, the mercy seat which covered it and on which he was manifested between the cherubim, and the altar of incense, the show-bread, and the lighted lamp before him ? As then, so now and evermore.

7. The Altar and the Laver suggest our need, and the need in all ages, of a purged conscience by the blood of sacrifice applied as it was to all parts of the tabernacle, as well as to the ministers at the altar; and the purification, not only of hands and feet, but of the

9

heart and life by the waters of regeneration and of personal holiness. The anointing oil is not only for Aaron but for the whole of the "holy nation."

8. The Tabernacle was outside of the camp. The world and the church must be separate. There was a Court in the Tabernacle for any and all; but the Court was not of the Camp, but of the Tabernacle. More than Moses stands in the door of the church and cries: " Who is on the Lord's side, let him come unto me."

9. They that truly come are the chosen, "the elect, precious," with whom alone the Lord's house is to be built.

10. In the days of the Tabernacle, by the eye was constantly taught the character and church-building of the ἀρχιτέκτων of human destiny as well of the material universe; in our day of the Gospel Church, how much more light may be acquired by prayerful study and godly living? Proper care of the Tabernacle, covering the ark as the human person contains the Lord as the hope of glory, was held as important as the observance of the Decalogue and the statutes of Moses. Is less care due the church? The right use of the ark and tabernacle brought blessing; the abuse, fearful cursing! What now of the use and abuse of the Lord's house? The Tabernacle was one of the three ante-christian pivotal points of human progress, the other two being the Ark and the Temple: all of them representing the human and divine building of the Carpenter's Son.

Moses' farewell address, which is the contents of the Book of Deuteronomy, is a wonderful record of all the divine building work in the wilderness, by one of the most wonderful men of the world's history. He died in Nebo, the Lord Jehovah alone with him. The Lord buried him. Of the dead man's body, we have, by the pen of Jude, this singular record : " Yet, Michael, the archangel, when contending with the devil, he disputed about the body of Moses, durst not bring against him a railing accusation, but said, the Lord rebuke thee."

His divinely written epitaph is : " And there arose not a prophet since like unto Moses, whom the Lord knew face to face. In all the signs and the wonders which the Lord sent him to do in the land of Egypt, to Pharaoh, and to all his servants, and to all his land, and in all that mighty hand, and in all the great terror which Moses showed in the sight of all Israel."

CHAPTER XVI.

SALIENT POINTS OF MOSAIC ECONOMY.

Without the shedding of blood there is no remission.—Heb. ix. 22.
Holiness becometh thy house, O Lord, forever.—Ps. xciii. 5.
Remember the Sabbath day to keep it holy.—Ex. xx. 8.
He that believeth not shall be damned.—Mark xvi. 16.

GLANCING over the legal system of Moses, the mind is struck with four prominent features, which it may be well, before progressing, to impress more deeply on the hearts of God's people, as builders of the Lord's house. I refer to the prominence given to Sacrifice, Holiness, The Sabbath, and Faith and Obedience, enforced by terrible retribution.

SACRIFICES.

The heart grows sick as it reads Leviticus—especially the first seventeen chapters. Blood, blood, blood—the burthen of the record; blood of dove, blood of kid, blood of sheep, blood of bullock; blood for priest, blood for prince, blood for peasant; blood for sin, blood for uncleanness, blood for leprosy—blood, blood, blood for everything. The spirit grows faint and is cast down. It asks: How can all this blood of burnt offering, and sin offering, and trespass offering and of all such offerings be a "sweet savor unto the Lord?" Let us note some points, and get cheer and comfort.

132

1. In Lev. xvii. blood is declared the life. Hence man is not to take blood; because blood or LIFE is devoted to God's altar, to make atonement for sin, which is death.

2. Everywhere we read, therefore, that "atonement" is made by priest in this blood of sacrifice, and sin is forgiven.

3. The idea is conveyed more clearly by the hand being put on the head of the victim, laying the sin of the sinner upon it, and then slaying it, and sending off free another animal into the wilderness.

4. This is declared a memorial "before the Lord." Memorial of what? Does it not bring to mind the lamb slain before the foundation of the world, because of which the sinner, man, is saved?

5. And memorial to us of the Lamb of Calvary, whose blood cleanseth from all guilt. That blood, how precious, how powerful, how plenteous! All this deluge of blood of the Jewish ritual is not too much to represent this blood—our only hope, our very holiness. The blood of lambs and goats was applied, in that day, to all persons and things that were holy unto the Lord; because this consecration can be secured alone now and ever by application of the blood of God's lamb.

6. The blood makes us not sick now. It is a gracious memorial—it is the world's panacea; it fills us with joy unspeakable. In all this blood we see most conspicuously "the Carpenter's Son," of whom it is written—"Christ died for the ungodly." We rejoice, because there is no remission without shedding of blood.

Remember the blood of beasts and birds did not take
away sin.

> Not all the blood of beasts,
>   On·Jewish altars slain,
> Could give the guilty conscience peace,
>   Or wash away the stain.
> But Christ, the heavenly Lamb,
>   Takes all our sins away ;
> A sacrifice of nobler name,
>   And richer blood than they.

HOLINESS.

No one can read chapters xviii. to xxii. of Leviticus,
with a prayerful heart and spiritual mind, without
being deeply affected. The intense earnestness of the
Lord for the perfect holiness of Israel, people as well
as priest, stands out in every passage. The constant
refrain is, I AM THE LORD. The iteration and reiter-
ation of this declaration gives awfulness to the commands and the prohibitions. This even is emphasized
in this book by the downright command, "Be ye holy ;
for I am holy." The holy God bringing man up to
himself as a standard of life and character is a thing
awfully solemn. The non-approach to Sinai, because
of God's presence, except to Moses and a few, impressed
the fearful holiness of the Lord God ; and now making
himself the standard of man's moral and spiritual self,
might well overwhelm the soul of spiritual insight,
reverence for the Most High, and longing for the perfection of his regenerated nature. This is the end of
the divine desire toward his people—their complete

holiness and consecration. "The will of God is our sanctification." The work of faith and sacrifice is to secure this great finality—conformity to the image of the Son of God, to which the children of Abraham are predestined. In a survey of the several economies of God, as discovered in his word, the Mind of Jehovah, on this momentous subject, seems thus :

1st. To require the most exhaustive outward cleanness and consecration ; and then,

2d. To demand the inward and the real holiness of which this outward cleanness and perfectness is the proper representation, if not symbol.

I. The first requirements we see under the Mosaic dispensation. There was required the most exacting scrupulosity as to cleanness and completeness as regards the person, and services, and circumstances, that it is possible to conceive, in connection with God's worship, and in the people of the Lord God. How many things defile; how much washing must be done; how many things disqualify from service at the altar; how careful the social relations to be; how terrible the penalties of violation; how suggestive that because the nations observe not these things they are spewed out of their lands! And especially the priests—their persons, their garments, their services—how clean, how holy, how consecrated! The Lord seems to exhaust his resources in the deep impression he makes of this necessity for his service.

II. And did not the mind and heart that cheerfully and joyfully and reverently complied with these positive

exactions indicate that faith and love and spirit of obedience which is the essence of the state required now for
the perfect service of the Lord? In a somewhat different way, Israel of old exhibited their mind to the
Lord; but so far as they conformed in spirit to these
laws, moral and ceremonial and social and political, they
indicated the essence of the heart that would be right
toward God in our day. In our dispensation, the faith
of the ancients is recorded, by many examples of it, to
stimulate the faith of the Church. The faith of the
harlot Rahab might, under the circumstances of our
day, have made her a burning and shining light in the
courts of our God.

III. At any rate, the spiritual exactions now are as
extreme as the ceremonial and social were, in the former
dispensation. In the gospel economy there are no "molten sea," no "lavers," no ten thousand requirements as
to the kind, and degree, and time of offering; no severe
prohibition of this and that and the other thing; the
lame, and blind, and deformed are not excluded from
official service of God's house. But, the simple command: "Be ye perfect as your Father, which is in heaven,
is perfect," covers infinitely more than all these Mosaic
laws as to personal cleanness, sincerity, holiness and
consecration. Every requirement of the ceremonial law
might be scrupulously performed, and the performer not
be fit for a doorkeeper in the house of the Lord. The
plowshare of the gospel must turn up the subsoil of the
soul and the imperishable seed of God imbedded so as
to bring forth the fruits of personal and ecclesiastical

godliness to find acceptance and favor and blessing in the sight of the Lord. As to sacrifice, blood, blood, blood, was the cry in ancient Israel; but, the blood of the gospel is infinitely more—the sacrifice inestimably greater. So as to holiness, the holiness of Israel of old was only the shadow of the holiness God demands now in his people. And the extreme ceremonial holiness of the priest is but an adumbration of the holiness demanded now of the least servant of the Most High as the holiness and work of the High Priest were only a picture of the holiness and sacred office of our Great High Priest who stands within the Holy of Holies of the heavenly Tabernacle. Read Leviticus and then the gospels; read the chapters from the 18th to the 22d, and then read the Sermon on the Mount. Thus may we be prostrated at the glory of our atoning Lord and the spiritual completeness required of the believer, on whose whole being should be inscribed, HOLINESS TO THE LORD.

THE SABBATH.

No service is so emphasized in the moral and ceremonial law as the Sabbath. Its binding obligation is repeated again and again and again. Its observance is clearly at the foundation of all perpetual religion. Remove this periodic service and convocation, and Israel goes back to paganism. Hence it is enforced by the most powerful considerations. And in view of the ultimate use of the Sabbath as commemorative of the foundation truth of the gospel, there is additional reason for its most stringent enforcement. A grand tribute to the Sabbath is made in the chapters of Leviticus from the 23d to the 28th. The great feast to be celebrated, the Passover, and feasts of harvests and Tabernacles, all involve the Sabbath and are reckoned by Sabbaths. They are called also "Convocations." These meetings for service to God make progress in the Lord's house. Now, they become frequent and permanently established, and are connected with the Sabbath. Thus they foreshadow the gospel economy. The more so, inasmuch as the offerings made to the Lord at these feasts must be sanctified by sacrifice. Here the blood again, just as all service now, is only acceptable through the merits of the crucified Jesus. But, the grandest and yet most awful testimony to the holiness with which the Lord regards the Sabbath, are the words he uses in connection with the most frightful punishment of his people—even the scattering and peeling them among the nations and the desolation of their lands. *Then*, he says, when the land is desolate and the people are dispersed, my Sabbaths shall be kept, for there will be none to desecrate it! Then *will there be rest*, because there shall be none to labor. There is an appalling satire in these words in Leviticus, 26th chapter, which should make an indelible impression as to God's sacred regard of that day. And the idea grows still more fearfully impressive, when the Lord Jehovah intimates that his Sabbaths being thus kept by the destruction of his people, he will remember his covenant with Abraham, and Isaac and Jacob, and have mercy on the remnant. In all sacred history, we recall no more awfully sublime vindication of a divine statute than this tribute to the

Sabbath. And does not human experience attest that God is not less jealous of his day now than then? How many can attest this truth :

> The Sabbath well spent
> Brings a week of content,
>   And strength for the toils of to-morrow.
> The Sabbath profaned,
> Whatever be gained,
>   Is a sure forerunner of sorrow.

FAITH, OBEDIENCE, RETRIBUTION.

The faith God requires is not half trust in him and half in ourselves or others. Like love, it is to be with all the mind and heart and strength. And in the enforcement of this vital law for man's restoration and his glory, God is no respecter of persons. Moses and Aaron were devoted servants. Again and again Moses cast himself on his face before the Lord for his people, and was the meekest of men, but he smote the rock at Meribah instead of speaking to it, with Aaron at his side ; and God makes Moses strip off Aaron's priestly garment and give it to another, that Aaron might die in Mt. Hor, as he himself was to die in Nebo. Neither can enter the land of promise because of the act at Meribah. The sons of Aaron were consumed because they burnt strange fire. Korah, his grandson, with his confederates who would be priests and princes, is swallowed up by the earth. Uzzah is slain in a subsequent period, because he would steady the tilting Ark. And the whole of the Israelites, except Joshua and Caleb, who did "the whole will of God," perish in the wilderness, though the Covenant with their fathers was kept by Jehovah. All this was to impress on the universe the absolute necessity of implicit obedience and unwavering faith. And how fearful the retribution for the sins of the nations! They are to be utterly exterminated—men, women and children. See the thirty-two thousand captive Midianite women slaughtered by order of Moses, because of the device, through them, of Balaam, to destroy the integrity, as they did, of the men of Israel. Oh, why, why? God is a glorious and gracious God. But his creatures who are to live forever must be taught the awful sinfulness of sin. Thus a few generations are sacrificed for the eternal good. Thus, too, the sacrifice of his Son may be better appreciated—the sin he bore and the sin from which the believer is relieved. In a grace-view God is love; in a sin-view "a consuming fire." How humbled should the soul be before him! And let not the believer boast that what he does has for it "Thus saith the Lord;" but rejoice that he does the THUS SAITH THE LORD.

CHAPTER XVII.

SETTLEMENT IN CANAAN.

I will give unto thee, and to thy seed after thee . . . all the land of
Canaan, for an everlasting possession.—Gen. xvii. 8.

THE conditions under which Israel entered Canaan, to
possess it as their country and home, were very favorable to success. In the first place, God had resolved to
drive out the peoples occupying the land because of their
wickedness. Their cup of iniquity was full, and God
had determined to destroy them. Hence the Lord told
Israel that it was not because of their righteousness that
these peoples should be dispossessed, but because of the
iniquity of these heathen. But, they should not be
driven out "in one year," said the Lord, "but little and
little," until Israel should have full possession. And a
goodly land was it that they were to possess, " Not as the
land of Egypt," said Moses, "whence ye came out,
where thou sowedst thy seed and wateredst it with thy
foot, as a garden of herbs: But, the land whither ye go
to possess it is a land of hills and valleys, and drinking
water of the rain of heaven: A land which the Lord
thy God careth for; the eyes of the Lord thy God are
always upon it, from the beginning of the year even
unto the end of the year." And may it not be that
other goodly lands are possessed by new races, not be-

cause they are righteous, but because the native inhabitants were wicked in the eyes of the Lord?

Besides this, Israel was a different people when they
entered Canaan from what they were when they came
out of Egypt, an unorganized mass of suddenly lib-
erated slaves. They had been brought under government, civil and religious, having rulers and judges over,
tens and hundreds and thousands. They had been
taught the most comprehensive principles of ethical
and religious truth, and had been given laws to regulate
every duty to God and every obligation to man. They
had been disciplined by varied and severe experience.
They had learned that man does not "live by bread
alone, but by every word that proceedeth out of the mouth
of God."   While they trusted the Lord God, "he bore
them as a father beareth his son," showing himself merciful and gracious; but, when they turned from him he
was revealed as a consuming fire. Moses prevailed
against Amalek while his heavy hands were stretched out.
And when he dishonored God by a hasty word he was
doomed not to enter the promised land. Yet the people
were assured that they should enter in because of the
promise to Abraham and Isaac and Jacob.   Neverthe-
less, none of the generation that came out of Egypt entered Canaan, save Joshua and Caleb.

In addition to this, just before they crossed the Jordan, Moses, reviewing for them the forty years in the
wilderness, presented to them, in a powerful manner, all
their duties and the most cogent considerations for per-
forming them.   He gives the obligations of the rulers

and the judges; and the obligations of the people, in the family, in the farm, in the mart, in the time of peace and in the time of war—obligations to the fellow-citizen and the stranger; to the freeman and the slave. Nor is there any circumstance or condition of life to which he does not apply the far-reaching principles and precepts of the divine law. All religious observances are detailed and enforced, especially the several great feasts which bring the people together in their joys and sadness before the Lord; and most specially the feast of the Passover, which he associates with the keeping of the Sabbath. In repeating the Ten Commandments, he adds to the fourth these words: "And remember that thou wast a servant in the land of Egypt and that the Lord thy God brought thee out thence through a mighty hand and by a stretched out arm: therefore the Lord thy God commanded thee to keep the Sabbath day." Again and again he begs them to "take heed" to themselves—not to forget that God humbled them in the wilderness that they might know themselves; and that he had been on his face twice for forty days and forty nights before the Lord because of their sins; to take heed to make no graven image of God, because they saw no "similitude" of Jehovah in the Mount; and to be faithful in all their worship, when God should choose a place for his name in the promised land. And, in order to make the deepest impression upon them, he not only composes a song, reminding them of their duties and their dangers, but he arranges a list of blessings and a list of curses, which are to be read to the congregated people alter-

nately from the sides of two opposing hills—showing
the abundant favors they would receive, if faithful to
the Lord God, and the terrible blastings that would come
upon them should they fall into the way of the heathen
and forget the living and true God.

But this was not all. The hosts were to be led into
this land by the valiant and experienced General
Joshua, who had no fear of man, but feared the living
God and had implicit faith in the God of Abraham,
and Isaac, and Jacob, who promised Canaan to the
children of Israel. It is written of him, in the wilderness : "Joshua, the son of Nun, a young man, departed
not out of the Tabernacle."

And yet further, they were to be preceded by the
Ark of the Covenant, wherein were the rod of God by
which the great miracles had been wrought, a pot of the
manna by which their lives had been sustained for four
decades of years, and the roll of God's word prepared
by the inspired pen of Moses. On that ark was to rest
hereafter the symbol of the Lord God, as ever present
with them.

But, lastly, this Lord God was present then in person. He had promised to go before them and "to fight
for them." In his song, Moses calls him their Rock,
which Paul interpreted as Christ. Referring to the
past defeat of their enemies the man of God sings :
"How should one chase a thousand and two put ten
thousand to flight except their Rock had sold them, and
the Lord had shut them up ? For their Rock is not as
our Rock, even our enemies themselves being judges."

He is the great Motive that the Man of God puts before them as his dying appeal, saying "that thou mayest fear this glorious and fearful name, THE LORD THY GOD !"

And may it not be that all the varied education, and experience, and discipline that God's people are now undergoing, and all the changes going on among the nations, and all the leadings of the faithful by the Providence of God are but conditions favorable for the hosts of Zion to go forth and possess the world promised as an inheritance, in the name and by the fear of that name, fearful and glorious, THE LORD OUR GOD?

In considering the actual settlement in Canaan by Israel, attention will be given mainly to the personal revelations to his people of the Lord God, who is Jehovah Jesus, and the common interest of the varied tribes in the worship of the same God, and in the same place, which is the most direct work of building the Lord's house, going up then as now under the superintendence of the Carpenter's Son.

IN THE DAYS OF JOSHUA.

The most signal personal appearance of the Lord, in those days, was before the City of Jericho. The inspired account is in these words: "And it came to pass when Joshua was by Jericho, that he lifted up his eyes and looked, and behold, there stood a man over against him with his sword drawn in his hand; and Joshua went unto him, and said unto him, Art thou for us or for our adversaries? And he said, Nay; but as Cap-

10

tain of the host of the Lord am I now come. And
Joshua fell on his face to the earth and did worship,
and said unto him, What saith my lord unto his servant? And the Captain of the Lord's host said unto
Joshua, Loose thy shoe from off thy foot; for the place
whereon thou standest is holy. And Joshua did so."
This is exactly the direction that the Lord God, who
appeared to Moses in Midian, said to that leader of
Israel: and this was the same Lord God who appears
to Joshua as "the Captain of the Lord's host." It was
he, therefore, that commanded the armies of Israel and
gave them all of their marvellous success; for he had
promised to go before them and to fight for them. It
was this same Jehovah Jesus that, on the eastern bank
of the Jordan, said to Joshua: "Now therefore arise,
go over this Jordan, thou and all this people; ... every
place that the sole of your foot shall tread upon, that
have I given unto you. ... Only be strong and very
courageous, that thou mayest observe to do according to
all the law which Moses my servant commanded thee.
... Thou shalt meditate therein day and night; ...
then thou shalt have good success." It was he that
went forward with the Ark of the Covenant which preceded the army of Israel in the dried-up Jordan, and
which followed the trumpeting priests around the walls
of Jericho, which fell flat; for it is written: "The
seven priests bearing the seven horns passed on before
the Lord, ... and the ark of the covenant of the Lord
followed them." It was he that ordered the circum-
cision and the sanctifying of the people and the cele-

bration of the Passover, and who, as it is said, "magnified Joshua in the sight of all Israel; and they feared him as they feared Moses all the days of his life." It was he who destroyed, by the hand of Joshua, the armies and cities and power of thirty-one kings, on the western side of the Jordan, as he had destroyed, by the hand of Moses, on the eastern side, Sihon, king of the Amorites, and Og, king of Bashan. It was he that "took the whole land, . . . and gave it for an inheritance unto Israel according to their divisions by the tribes. And the land rested from war."

But of this personal presence of Jehovah, several remarks may be made:

1. It was not vouchsafed, with such glorious results, except on the condition of implicit obedience. When Achan violated the command that "all the silver and gold and vessels of brass and iron shall be consecrated unto the Lord," the Captain of the host forsook Israel, and they were disgracefully defeated by the inhabitants of Ai. And in order to enforce obedience essential to his presence, Achan and all his family were mercilessly stoned, and, with all his property, consumed by fire. The reason assigned for the great success of Joshua is that "he left nothing undone of all that the Lord commanded Moses."

2. This personal presence of Jehovah did not take the place of providence and good generalship on the part of Joshua. After the destruction of Achan, and "the Lord turned from the fierceness of his anger," the Captain of the host ordered Joshua to go up against

Ai, and he went up, not with three thousand men, but with "30,000;" and he "lay in ambush behind the city," and utterly destroyed it and all the inhabitants thereof, "both men and women, 12,000," and made it "a heap forever, even a desolation unto this day."

3. And this presence was for the utter destruction of these people of Canaan, whose cup of iniquity seemed full. He cursed the man that should ever re-build Jericho; his usual order was that in the destruction of these people "nothing should be left that has breath." Their utter extermination was required. Though merciful and gracious to his friends, to his adversaries he is, indeed, a "consuming fire."

4. And does not this personal presence indicate the great care the Lord has over his people whom he would have settled in this land of promise "decently and in order," and according to his promise to Abraham, Isaac, and Jacob?

(1) The bones of the noble Joseph are not lost, but are safely deposited in the sepulchre of his father.

(2) The inheritance of his children is given to them before the lots are cast, as was the inheritance of the elect Judah, whose portion is said to have been "too much."

(3) The lots cast were no doubt directed by the Lord, and thus the whole land was rightly and wisely divided out among the children of Israel.

And most significant is it that these children of Israel elected as builders of the Lord's house among the nations, should, despite their bloody wars, have their minds and hearts so fixed upon this work of giving honor to the Lord.

1. They erect a memorial of the miraculous passage of Jordan at Gilgal.

2. At Mount Ebal they build an Altar to the Lord and inscribed it with the Decalogue received on Mount Sinai : and from Ebal and Gerizim, the blessings and cursings of God, commanded by Moses, are read in the presence of the host and people.

3. To the Levites whose inheritance was "the sacrifices of the Lord God of Israel made by fire " the tribes give out of their portions " forty and eight cities with their suburbs."

4. Shiloh is established as the seat of the ark, and the altar, and the tabernacle, and the divine presence, and congregated worship of the Lord God ; and most zealous are the tribes for the honor of their God. When Reuben, Gad, and the half tribe of Manasseh, after being exhorted by Joshua "to take diligent heed to do the commandment and the law . . . to love the Lord your God and to walk in all his ways . . . and to serve him with all your heart and with all your soul," went away to enter into their possession, on the other side of the Jordan, and there built " a great altar," after the pattern of the one at Shiloh, all the other tribes rose in arms against them, and fearful fratricidal war would have ensued, had not these tribes protested before God, in the most solemn manner, that the altar was not for sacrifice but to instruct their children with regard to the altar and tabernacle of their Lord God at Shiloh.

" And the thing pleased the children of Israel : and the children of Israel blessed God, and did not incline to go up against them in battle to destroy the land wherein the children of Reuben and Gad dwelt. And the children of Reuben and the children of Gad called the altar *Ed :* for it shall be a witness between us that the Lord is God."

5. So careful are they of the divine honor that, Rahab and her house are saved because she hid the spies, believing that the Lord would give her land to Israel ; the Gibeonites were not only spared from the common destruction, because Israel, though deceived by them, had sworn peace unto them, but Israel went up against their enemies ; for the slaughter of whom Joshua commanded the Sun to stop upon Gibeon and the moon in the valley of Ajalon. "And there was no day like that day before it or after it, that the Lord hearkened unto the voice of a man; for the Lord fought for Israel." Special mention is made of the burial of Eleazar, for he was " the son of Aaron," the priest. And special inheritances are given to Caleb and Joshua, because of their peculiar fidelity to the Lord—having " WHOLLY FOLLOWED THE LORD OUR GOD."

6. And when Joshua, Moses-like, made his farewell address to the people, the burden of it was that they should be faithful to the Lord God. He tempted them, saying, " Ye cannot serve the Lord ; for he is a holy God." But, they protested, " Nay, but we will serve the Lord." With sad remembrance of the fate of the hundreds of thousands who fell in the wilderness because

of their unbelief, Joshua warns them, "If ye forsake the Lord, and serve strange gods, then he will turn and do you hurt and consume you after he hath done you good ;" but they vowed " the Lord our God will we serve, and his voice will we obey." "So Joshua made a covenant with the people that day, and set them a statute and an ordinance in Shechem . . And Israel served the Lord all the days of Joshua and all the days of the elders that outlived Joshua, and which had known all the works of the Lord that he had done for Israel."

But, Israel is not so careful of the honor and glory of the Lord God as he himself is. Not only was this settlement of Israel in Canaan for the building of the house of the Lord, but the terrific destruction of these peoples inhabiting the land, was for the glory of his name. These passages are worthy of note : " For it was of the Lord to harden their hearts that they should come against Israel in battle that he might destroy them utterly, and that they might have no favor, but that he might destroy them as the Lord commanded Moses, ... that all the people might know the hand of the Lord that it is mighty ; that ye might fear the Lord your God forever."

And from these facts, may not the people of God, in our day, seeking the possession of the world in the name of the Lord and for the building of his house, learn some valuable and essential lessons, with regard to the presence of the Carpenter's Son, who said : " And lo ! I am with you alway, even unto the end of the world. Amen."

CHAPTER XVIII.

IN THE DAYS OF THE JUDGES.

And when the Lord raised them up judges, then the Lord was with the judge.—Judges xi. 18.

IN the days of Joshua the Lord God did not drive out all the inhabitants from the land of Canaan, though the whole land was divided out among the tribes of Israel. The destruction had been immense, but many of these heathen were left designedly in the land, as the Lord declared, "to prove" Israel; and, if they proved unworthy, to be "thorns and snares" unto them. After the death of Joshua the children of Israel cried unto the Lord because of the Canaanites, and the Lord God appeared unto the elect Judah and bade his tribe to go up against the adversary, and with the assistance of Simeon they went up, and Jerusalem was taken and ten thousand of the Canaanites and Perizzites were put to the sword. And fearful retribution was visited upon Adonibezek, "the lord of lightning,"—under whose table seventy kings with thumbs and great toes cut off had "gathered their meat,"—by cutting off his thumbs and great toes; so that he said, "as I have done, so God hath requited me." And now it is significantly written, "And the Lord was with Judah, and he drave out the inhabitants of the mountain; but could not drive out the inhabi-

152

tants of the valley, because they had chariots of iron."
Could not the Lord God overthrow chariots of iron?
Here comes in a sad story. All the days of Joshua,
and of the elders of his day, the people served the
Lord, and he, according to promise, was with them for
the upbuilding of his house and worship of truth. But,
alas, the Lord God after that forsakes them, according
to his word, for "there arose another generation after"
the generation of Joshua's time had been gathered to
their fathers, "which knew not the Lord, nor yet the
works which he had done in Israel." And what was
the cause of this? Read: "The children of Israel
dwelt among the Canaanites, Hittites, and Amorites
and Perizzites, and Hivites and Jebusites: and they
took their daughters to be their wives, and gave their
daughters to their sons, and served their gods. And
the children of Israel did evil in the sight of the Lord,
and forgat the Lord their God, and served Baalim and
the groves." And the consequence has been anticipated.
According to the warnings of Joshua and Moses, and
the repeated declarations of Jehovah, he forsook them.
He forsook them when they ceased to build his house,
and began to build the house of Baalim, whose altars
and groves they had been straitly ordered to overthrow
and destroy, with the wicked worshippers themselves.
When Moses came down from Sinai and saw the
idolatry of the people, he stood by the tabernacle and
cried: " Who is on the Lord's side? let him come unto
me;" and then he put the idolaters to the sword.
Thus he emphasized the Lord's hatred of such wicked-

ness. And Joshua also said, before he died: "Choose you this day whom ye will serve. As for me and my house, we will serve the Lord." And the people cried out, "God forbid that we should forsake the Lord to serve other gods!" And yet, here they are at the feet of Baal! And terrible judgment came: they are subjected at one time eight years to the king of Mesopotamia; at another, eighteen years to the king of Moab; and, again, twenty years to Jabin, king of the Canaanites, besides long periods to the Philistines. But the people repented of their folly, and in their agonies cried unto the God of Abraham and Isaac and Jacob, and he remembered his covenant with the fathers. "And the Spirit of the Lord came upon Othniel," and he prevailed against Chushan-rishathaim, "and the land had rest for forty years." And the Lord raised up Ehud, who assassinated the fat Eglon, while saying to him, "I have a message from God unto thee," and overthrew Moab; "and the land had rest for eighteen years." Then arose the prophetess Deborah, *before whom the Lord went;* and the bold Jael, Heber's wife. By the wisdom of the one and the nail and hammer of the other, Sisera and his host came to naught: the history of which is graphically sung in "The Song of Deborah and Barak." Then had the land rest for forty years.

But, alas, alas, Israel proved themselves "the stiffnecked" people that the Lord told them they were, and soon "the Midianites and Amorites and children of the east" overspread the land "as grasshoppers for multitude," so that there was "left no sustenance for Israel, neither sheep, nor ox, nor ass." Fearful was their plight as they were driven from their fields and houses into "caves and dens and strongholds" in the mountains, because of the Midianites. But, the Lord God is to be entreated by the children of men, and marvellous is his patience and grace. Herein is he identified perfectly with the Carpenter's Son of Nazareth. Such endurance, such mercy, such loving-kindness, could only exist in one—the infinitely good, the Lord God of Israel. And, in response to the agonies of his again repentant people, he comes down and sits under an oak in Ophrah and has a marvellous interview with Gideon, the son of Joash the Abi-ezrite. Gideon looked like "the son of a king," and was "a mighty man of valor;" but, he was more than that; he was a humble man and a man of mighty faith. His interview with Jehovah reminds us of the interviews with him of Abraham and Joshua. Three great miracles he extorts from the Almighty in attestation of his being the God of his fathers. Then he begins the work on the Lord's house, overthrowing the altar of Baal and destroying his groves; erects an altar to the living and true God; goes forth with three hundred men and slaughters one hundred and twenty thousand warriors, slaying their kings with his own hand; and then, to the demand of Israel, "Rule thou over us, both thou and thy son, and thy son's son also," he grandly replies, "I will not rule over you, neither shall my son rule over you: THE LORD SHALL RULE OVER YOU." Thus was Midian subdued, "and the country was in quietness forty years in the days of Gideon."

But time goes on and again we read: "And it came to pass as soon as Gideon was dead that the children of Israel turned again and went a whoring after Baalim and Baal-berith their god." This opens up a view of the sad state of fallen human nature that makes us smite upon our breast, pity our fellow men, bewail the nations of the earth, and justify God in all his judgments among the children of men. Now the presence and mercy of the Lord seem clean gone forever. The Philistines come down and oppress them, and they cry again to the Lord, but he responds, "Go and cry unto the gods which ye have chosen: let them deliver you in the time of your tribulation." And fearful beyond description was the state of things, with occasional reliefs from the face and hand of Jehovah, from the days of Gideon to the days of Samuel, the judge and prophet and man of God. Of some of the judges it is only written that they had so many sons who rode on so many "ass colts;" and the dismal record appears, here and there, " In those days there was no king in Israel: every man did that which was right in his own eyes." But, what was "right in his own eyes," was for the most part fearfully wrong in the eyes of God. Gideon's son, Abimelech, slaughters the whole of his father's house (save one), "threescore and ten persons on one stone;" and has his own skull righteously crushed by a piece of millstone from the hand of a woman in the tower of Thebez; and was worthily sung by his brother Jotham's parable of the Bramble. This was the beginning of a period of darkness and horror which

was marked by the chapter of Benjamin's appalling
deed, that made even the God-forsaken brother tribes to
rise up and put to death twenty-five thousand of their
name, which virtually wiped out the tribe of Benjamin
from the tribes of the children of Israel. Yet the Lord
God was not without witnesses even in this dark age. He
appeared unto Jephthah,—though he reflected his times
by his reckless and fatal vow,—who discussed bravely the
rights of Israel's possessions with the king of Ammon
and then put his hosts to the sword for troubling the
Lord's people. The Almighty τέκτων talked face to face
with Manoah and his wife, giving them a marvellous sign
of the presence of the Lord God; and his Spirit came
mightily upon their mighty son, who avenged his people's
wrongs upon the Philistines, while enveloping himself in
darkness and ruin. But no picture of the times, with
regard to the damage to the Lord's house, is darker than
the one of which an insight is obtained by "the ephod,
and teraphim, and graven and molten images" of the
house of Micah in Mount Ephraim, and his Levite priest,
because of which he said, "Now know I that the Lord
will do me good;" by the stealing of all of them by
the children of Dan, that they might be unto them in
the place of Shiloh and the Lord God; by the elders of
the congregation of Israel inducing men of Benjamin
to capture for wives the girls dancing at the yearly feast
of the Lord at Shiloh; and especially by the awful cor-
ruption in the family of the aged priest Eli, which
ended in the ark being taken by impious hands from
Shiloh and captured by the Philistines, while the sons

of the old man, who carried it forth, are slain, the old man's neck is broken and thirty thousand of Israel are slain. "Ichabod" is the name given to Eli's grandson, which means, "The glory of the Lord is departed." The Ark of the Covenant is carried about by horrid, uncircumcised enemies, inflicting destruction on them and on their God, and is then driven out of their land in an unguided ox cart, to rest on the road not less than twenty years from the house of the Lord. Alas, for Israel! They were indeed a God-forsaken people; and the Lord's spiritual house was well nigh in ruins.

But a gleam of hope for the Lord's house comes from that gem of Israel's history, Ruth, as we see her clinging to Naomi in Moab, and coming to Bethlehem of Judah, saying: "Thy people shall be my people and thy God my God;" when we hear Boaz saluting his reapers, "The Lord be with you," and them returning the salutation, "The Lord bless thee;" when we listen to the olden time words of the people that are in the gate and the elders, "We are witnesses. The Lord make the woman that is come into thine house like Rachel and like Leah, which two did build the house of Israel; and do thou worthily in Ephratah, and be famous in Bethlehem; And let thy house be like the house of Pharez, whom Tamar bare unto Judah, of the seed which the Lord shall give thee of this young woman;" and when, finally we read, "There is a son born to Naomi; and they called his name Obed; he is the father of Jesse, the father of David."

And we get into the dawning light when we come to the last and noblest of Israel's judges, the godly Samuel. He was a child of prayer, and the child of godly parents, whom the Lord God directly visited, and unto whom the child was vowed, and was given for life, as a servant of the Lord's house so soon as he was "weaned." To Samuel the Lord God appeared; by him the aged Eli was warned and his doom announced because he restrained not the sacrilegious vileness of his sons who served the altar; by him were the people led to repentance and the renewal of the worship of the Lord God; by him did the Lord do a great wonder in the sight of the people and the Philistines; and by him "the Philistines were subdued, and they came no more in the coast of Israel." And all the cities which had been taken from Israel, "from Ekron even unto Gath," were recaptured, and Israel was delivered "out of the hands of the Philistines." And at Ramah, Samuel "built an altar unto the Lord." Yet the people rebelled, and demanded a king. And the Lord God told Samuel that the people did not thereby reject the Lord's servant, but the Lord God himself whom they would not have to rule over them, and that he must anoint Saul their king. Samuel obeys the Lord, after warning the people of the consequence of their folly. And the old Judge and Prophet lives long enough to see Saul put sacrilegious hand on the altar at Shiloh, and to lie unto God in the matter of saving the best of the flocks and cattle of the conquered King of Amalek, whom also Saul saved, contrary to God's command, but whom

Samuel, in holy wrath, hewed to pieces with his own hand.   The conduct of Saul grieved Samuel so greatly that he cried all night before the Lord.   And before he was honorably gathered to his fathers, he gave these words of sound wisdom and of deep insight into human and divine nature, to the people.   And Samuel said unto the people, "Fear not; ye have done all this wickedness: yet turn not aside from following the Lord, but serve the Lord with all your heart; and turn ye not aside: for then should ye go after vain things, which cannot profit nor deliver; for they are vain.   For the Lord will not forsake his people for his great name's sake: because it hath pleased the Lord to make you his people.   Moreover, as for me, God forbid that I should sin against the Lord in ceasing to pray for you; but I will teach you the good and the right way: only fear the Lord, and serve him in truth with all your heart; for consider how great things he hath done for you.   But, if ye shall still do wickedly, ye shall be consumed, both ye and your king."

Greatly zealous was the old man for the honor of God's house; and he had the consolation of anointing a successor to Saul, even "a man after God's heart,"— the son of Jesse,—whose zeal for God's house was so great that he was honored by a son whose mission in life was to erect the magnificent temple at Jerusalem, in which city of the Lord David had brought the Ark of the Covenant, after its separation from the Lord's house for twenty years in Kirjath-jearim.

RETROSPECTIVE VIEW.

The question arises, What progress has been made, up to this time, in the building of the Lord's house? In answering the question, it must be borne in mind that the house of the Lord is spiritual, and is built by the establishment of truth in the minds of his intelligent creatures, of right principles in their hearts, of worshipful conduct in their lives, and of all those ways which may be ultimately subordinated to the edification of the great spiritual structure.

I.   Among God's people it was established:

1. That, though salvation is by grace, the presence and blessing of the Lord cannot be enjoyed without personal piety and the worship of his name where his name is recorded.   Religion must be localized.

2. That the possessions which may be by grace can only be acquired by great struggle, and retained in the same way.

3. That the heart is deceitful above all things and desperately wicked, and cannot be trusted : but all trust must be put in the Lord.

4. That the promises of Jehovah may be relied upon, but there may be a presumptuous reliance which can have only a fatal consequence.

5. That, though there is much evil among God's people, in all ages there are those who fear God and walk uprightly and are manifestly the heirs of eternal life.

II. Among the nations:

1. It was established that man is a sinner and that
11

the way of the transgressor is hard, because he is under the righteous displeasure of God.

2. It was established that the human heart must have some God, though it may not find peace in any but the living and true God.

3. The varied forms of worship among the nations established human nature in active service of a religious sort: his houses erected, his altars built, his groves planted for his God, showed man to be an essential builder; which builder naturally inclines to building for the Most High, and may be turned, in time, to this end, by the power of his might.

4. That all his advancement in art and science and wealth, and all his possessions belong to the Lord, and may be, from time to time, turned over to the worshippers of the true God, as the land of Canaan was given to the children of Israel.

5. That Israel and Canaan may be a picture of the world's future history.

These were some of the truths taught, up to this time, by the Lord God among the children of men, and they are vital elements in the construction of his house, which had thus made no little progress on the earth. And no truth, it may be added, was more clearly manifested both in Israel and among the nations than that the house of the Lord God building on earth, by his personal presence, is obstructed, in every possible way, by the personal presence of the great destroyer of man and God's works, the devil, with his angels. This fact accounts for much we have seen in Israel and among the nations.

CHAPTER XIX.

IN THE DAYS OF THE KINGS.

And the Lord said . . . they have rejected me, that I should not reign over them.—1 Sam. viii. 7.

IN these days much progress was made in the work of the τέχτων, or ὁ ἀρχιτέχτων, by the practical illustration of great doctrines and the exemplification of important characters, all for the advantage of the kingdom of heaven. Among the doctrines illustrated were these:

1. That man is not to be a law to himself. His will cannot be supreme. He may reject God as his ruler, as Israel did, but he must not rule himself. Saul was only a sample of the kings of the world. The people under them are well called subjects. And man should be subject to some higher power. The family organization is designed to teach practically this important lesson; and the governments of the world, especially the kingdoms, teach this more fully. The nature of man is thus trained, even under bad government, and thus becomes better fitted for the government of God. The essence of sin is self-will; and the kingdoms of the world tend to the suppression of this essential evil of mankind. Hence, it is written that the Magistrate is a "minister of God," and does not wield the sword in vain.

2. Another doctrine was that whatever the conditions and changes among men, they are all overruled for the glory of God. All the courses and wars of the kingdom of Israel, as well as of the surrounding and the most distant nations, were all according to natural laws, and yet they were all serving the great purposes of Jehovah. Even the wrath of men he makes to praise him and the remainder of wrath he restrains.

3. The division of God's House under Jeroboam and Rehoboam was a great sin, but the establishment of two centres for worship illustrated what the Carpenter's Son declared, in his day, that the worship of God, who is a Spirit, is not confined to any locality, but may be conducted wherever he is called upon in spirit and in truth. This great doctrine was also illustrated by the destruction of Jerusalem, because of the wickedness of Kings and people.

4. And the captivity itself illustrated the great doctrine that God's people have important relations with the peoples of the world. Israel's ideas were expanded by his captivity in Egypt, and more so by the Babylonian captivity. And good was done to both of their foreign masters. Egypt learned lessons from the Lord God never to be forgotten; and so did Babylon. The Lord God was no more signally present in the courts of David and Solomon than he was in the Courts of Nebuchadnezzar, Belshazzar, Ahasuerus and Cyrus. Daniel and Ezekiel were his mouthpiece in the Captivity as plainly as were Elijah and Elisha in Jerusalem and Samaria. The Lord God was no nearer to the King of

Israel when he talked to him, face to face, at the thresh-
ing-place of Araunah, the Jebusite, than he was to the
Hebrew children in the fiery furnace, where he appeared,
even to·pagan eyes, as "the Son of God." The heads of
these nations were "stirred up" by him, and directed
by him, for the upbuilding of his house, just as the
Kings of Judah and of Israel were. This fact should
draw out the minds of God's people toward the nations,
in more earnest consideration than they are often drawn
out. If the heathen seem God-forsaken, it is just as
Saul, Israel's first King, was forsaken of the Lord God.

And important characters were exemplified under the
Kings, for the permanent advantage of the Lord's
house. Many of the several classes, formalists, heart-
worshippers and practical workers, might be cited from
the long list of Kings of Judah and Israel, but let one
of each class suffice for the lasting consideration of God's
people, while building the house of the Lord. The
three first kings happen to be good exemplifications of
these three classes.

1. Saul was an essential formalist. There was much
that was admirable in him. He was handsome, modest
and seemingly reverential. The Spirit of God also
came upon him, and in a certain sense "gave him another heart." He prophesied in the name of God, and
"built an altar" to his name. But, whenever the test
came, it became apparent that "the root of the matter"
was not in him. He goes to Shiloh to counsel with God
before going out to battle; but, contrary to the first principles of God's worship, he himself serves at the altar,

because Samuel is not present at the expected moment. Amalek is accursed of God and is to be annihilated, according to God's word, and his substance with him ; but Saul not only spares Agag, but brings back the flocks and herds under the pretext that they are for the altar of the Lord God. Under the influence of the godly Samuel, the witch and wizard are suppressed in the land ; but, Samuel dead, the King goes to the witch of Endor to bring back the old man to life ! But, the prophet asks, "Why consult me when forsaken of God ? " Now left to himself, Saul is possessed of the evil spirit ; and the aim of his life seems to be the murder of David, the Lord's anointed and his own best friend. And despite all his pretense of serving the Lord, he miserably perishes by the hand of the enemy, according to the word of Samuel and the decree of the Lord God. This lesson has a wide application, and its presentation in Israel's history may have influenced myriads to guard against the defect of this servant of God; whom God made a builder of the Lord's house; the exposure of his hypocrisy was an illustrious warning to God's people.

2. David was a character just the opposite. Like Saul, he had natural advantages. He was of goodly person ; he was cultured in music and poetry. He was as brave as a lion, being more than a match for the lion or the bear, and for Goliath too ! He was loving-hearted and most magnanimous, as witnessed by his devotion to Jonathan, and his repeated sparing of Saul's life. More than that, he even avenged Saul's death by slaying the

young man that ended the royal suicide's misery and brought his crown to David ; kept Saul's grandson at the King's table, and celebrated, in eloquent song, the Lord's fallen anointed and his far nobler son. But, this was not David's excellence. Saul might have been all that and yet might have miserably perished. The excellence of David was that the Spirit of God was in his heart, and he was truly and constantly zealous for the Lord's glory. In all of his movements of state or of war, his soul seemed to look instinctively to the Lord, as "the man of his counsel." He takes Jerusalem, and fetches the ark to " the city of the Lord," with such personal rejoicing that he brings upon himself the contempt of his wife, the daughter of Saul. But, his life was to be right, not merely in the sight of men, as was her father's, but in the sight of God. In all the vast complications of his life, from the time he left the sheep of his father until he was gathered to his fathers, his walk was wise and his spirit was full of the fragrance of truth and justice and mercy and heaven —save in two fearful exceptions! But, in these crimes he shows himself a man of God. For numbering Israel, he throws himself into the arms of divine mercy, and, talking face to face with Jehovah about his sin, submits to the divine judgment and makes a sin offering for his guilt. About the black matter of Bathsheba, the best notice is the 51st Psalm, which, until the end of time, will be at once the best evidence of David's contrition, and the fittest expression of penitence that the sinner can ever make. That Psalm has done

more good in building God's house than perhaps the
same number of lines ever written by any sinner's
pen. And the Psalms, as a collection, are the best
history of the godly experience of this godly man,
whom Samuel declared was "after God's own heart."
And perhaps there never was a soul more desirous
of showing his love and gratitude by building the
Lord's house than David. His delight was to dwell
in the house of the Lord; and he would erect a
Temple for him worthy of his name. Forbidden of
the Lord to do it in person, he makes the most munificent provisions for his son and successor to do it. This
was the burden of his charge to Solomon that he should
perform faithfully this work. And if any distinction
can be made in the songs of the " sweet singer of Israel,"
those seem the most charming that relate to the services
of God's house, as for instance, his " psalms of degrees."
And when we think of the universal use of these songs
among God's people of every age, the estimate of this
one item of David's life, for the edification of the saints,
seems altogether beyond calculation. And an appropriate finale of David's life-long sentiment, "One thing
have I desired of the Lord, and that I will seek after.
That I may dwell in the house of the Lord all the days
of my life to behold the beauty of the Lord and to inquire
in his temple," may be found in the following passage
taken from the latter part of his life, and showing his
intense zeal for the Lord's house : " Then David said,
This is the house of the Lord God, and this is the altar
of the burnt offering for Israel. And David com-

manded to gather together the strangers that were in the land of Israel ; and he set masons to hew wrought stones to build the house of God. And David prepared iron in abundance for the nails for the doors of the gates, and for the joinings : and brass in abundance without weight; also cedar trees in abundance : for the Zidonians and they of Tyre brought much cedar wood to David. And David said, Solomon my son is young and tender, and the house that is to be builded for the Lord must be exceeding magnifical of fame and glory throughout all countries : I will therefore now make preparation for it. So David prepared abundantly before his death. Then he called Solomon his son and charged him to build a house for the Lord God of Israel. And David said to Solomon˙ . . . Now my son, the Lord be with thee ; and prosper thee and build the house of the Lord thy God, as he hath said of thee. Only the Lord give thee wisdom and understanding, and give thee charge concerning Israel, that thou mayest keep the law of the Lord thy God. . . Be strong and of good courage; dread not nor be dismayed. Now, behold, in my trouble, I have prepared for the house of the Lord a hundred thousand talents of gold, and a thousand thousand talents of silver ; and of brass and iron without weight; for it is in abundance : timber also and stone have I prepared; and thou mayest add thereto. Moreover, there are workmen with thee in abundance, hewers and workers in stone and timber, and all manner of cunning men for every manner of work. Of the gold and silver and the brass and the iron there is no number. Arise, therefore, and be doing, and the Lord be with thee. David also commanded all the princes of Israel to help Solomon his son, saying, Is not the Lord your God with you? and hath he not given you rest on every side? for he hath given the inhabitants of the land into thine hand; and the land is subdued before the Lord, and before his people. Now set your heart and your soul to seek the Lord your God; arise, therefore, and build ye the sanctuary of the Lord God, to bring the ark of the Covenant of the Lord, and the holy vessels of God, into the house that is to be built in the name of the Lord. So when David was old and full of days, he made Solomon his son king of Israel."

3. Solomon illustrates the practical worker in the house of the Lord. We need not refer to his magnificent gifts, his boundless wealth, his superlatively splendid surroundings, his world-wide fame that brought to his Court the wisest and most distinguished of the world. And, by the way, Solomon illustrated also that the greatness of wisdom and wealth is not great enough to keep the soul from falling into hideous sin! "Not by might nor power, but by my Spirit, saith the Lord." But, for David's sake and God's covenant with him, Solomon would have been forsaken of God. This is the divine testimony. But, instead of his being the world's wreck of wisdom and wealth, he stands out as the church's inspiration to subordinate all possible means for the edification of God's house. We need not refer here to the cost, the magnificence of Solomon's Temple—"the joy

of the whole world." That was merely external. The great work that Solomon did was to crystallize into one grand ritual every element of true worship which had been developed by the Lord God from the beginning of the world unto his day, thus making visible and permanent and representative what was taught in God's word and foreshadowed in the Tabernacle. Solomon built in stone and cedar and gold a model of the kingdom of God on earth and in heaven. He was God's agent of focalizing all the elements of the divine essence and purpose and practice and government among men into a splendid adumbration of the Lord's universal and everlasting kingdom of ransomed souls. How appropriate that, after its dedication," the glory of the Lord filled the house." Solomon was a practical worker, while, as we have seen, something more than that. Would there were more in God's house! But, better would it have been had Solomon prayed more as his father did. Let the two go hand in hand. Let the heart be ever near to God that Solomon's sin may be shunned; and let the hand, with all its circumstance and possible help, be in the Lord's work that Solomon's work may prove itself a holy inspiration.

It need not be added that the Lord God was present with these his servants. This is repeatedly stated. He sends down fire from heaven in answer to David's prayer, and talks with Solomon in the visions of the night. And how else could their great works for his house have been done? And all his manifestations proved him the same as " the Carpenter's Son."

Other kings might be cited, both for warning and for inspiration—kings, as Ahab and Ahaz, who, like Saul, dishonored God, and kings like David, as Josiah and Hezekiah, that gave great honor to his name. And not only kings. Many holy men and women, in these days of the kings, worked well and marvellously under the inspiration of the ubiquitous Carpenter's Son. And fearful was his vengeance on his adversaries! By the prayer of one man of God, one hundred and eighty-five thousand investing adversaries perish in a night. Such men as Isaiah, and Jeremiah, and Elijah and Elisha were almost impersonations—with human frailties—of the Divine presence itself! And in the captivity, Ezekiel, and Daniel, and Nehemiah, and Ezra and the rest of the great builders of the Lord's house! And how powerful was the divine presence among the heathen—avenging the injury of God's elect, and inspiring to the Lord's glory! How plainly the Carpenter's Son was near the heart of the Persian monarch, who through Esther saves his people; and through Nehemiah and Ezra repeats the grand work that Solomon did. The reorganization of God's house in Jerusalem is one of the sublimest passages in human history. Nehemiah seems a well-nigh perfect son of God—a model man for all ages, and most distinguished for his love for, and his building of, the Lord's house. He stands under the old economy, as Paul stands under the new. *Par nobile fratrum:* the world's inspiration as builders of the house of the Lord God.

And let it be added that the best exposition of the

house that Nehemiah and Solomon built is given to the Hebrews by the Apostle Paul. As Abraham's seed is condensed in one word, so is the Lord's house; and that word is the same, "Christ," which is identical with "the Carpenter's Son."

CHAPTER XX.

THE TEMPLE.

WITH PRESENT LESSONS TO GOD'S PEOPLE.

Know ye not that ye are the temple of God, and that the Spirit of God dwelleth in you?—1 Cor. iii. 16.

IN deriving lessons for God's people from the temple, it may be viewed externally and internally.

I. *Externally*, as to its stability, its multitude of builders, its costliness, and as an object of love and source of influence.

1. In comparison with the Tabernacle, the Temple was a structure so substantial that it might have seemed everlasting. Its foundations, despite the changes of time, stand until this day, and may stand until "the last day." Thus was depicted the permanence of God's spiritual house. It is based upon the principles of eternal truth, which are embedded in the mind and heart and conscience of God's servants, past, present and to come; and their being would have to be exterminated to overthrow the foundations of the Lord's house. Yea, it is founded on the very being of the everlasting God. The house of Baal, of Mahomet, of Buddha, of Brahma, may seem steadfast; but, as the Ark of the Covenant overthrew Dagon in his house of worship, as the stone cut out of the mountain without

174

hands overthrew the great image, so shall all the houses of idols and false gods be overthrown. And as that stone cut out of the mountain filled the whole earth, so shall the Lord's house be based upon the universal acceptance of its truth and of its God; and how can it be otherwise than everlasting?

2. The numbers engaged in the erection of the temple were very great. Of a certain class of workmen—"hewers and burden-bearers"—it is said that their number was one hundred and fifty thousand, with thirty-six hundred overseers. How many more must they have been in all? And these workmen were both Jews and Gentiles. It is a significant fact that David employed "strangers" to prepare the material in his day; and Solomon, in erecting the house, calls to his assistance the king of a heathen nation. But what were these numbers to the multitudes who have been, and are presently, and who shall be employed on the erection of God's house? The number is such that "no man can number." The builders are of every age and every clime. Even the nations most remote now from the work shall be gathered in and become co-workers with the Lord in the erection of this house, for which all things were made. Some idea of the aggregate number we get at when we note the expressions of multitude made in the Apocalypse of John. But, enough; "no man can number" them.

3. And what of the cost of the Temple? David said he had laid aside for the building "over and above all that I have prepared for the house of the

Lord, . . . of mine own proper good three thousand talents of gold of Ophir and seven thousand talents of refined silver." This, of itself, would amount to some $89,000,000. But that was only a part of the cost, which has been estimated at some four billions of our money! But, costly as the Temple of Solomon was, more costly is the spiritual house of the Lord.

(1) To man it is to cost the wealth and knowledge and intellect of the race.

(2) To nature, all its works.

(3) To God it has already cost the life of his Son.

4. But how loved was the Temple to the Jewish heart? There was the Shekinah; there, his sin-offering; there, his hope; there, his all. Even the destruction of it could not destroy his love for it and its power over him. In captivity he cried: "If I forget thee, O Jerusalem!" So the heart of God's people must be wrapped up in the house of the Lord. There is surely their all; for there is their Saviour and their God! And thus is the Lord's house to have the influence and power to absorb every means that can be employed in its erection, in the workman; and to send him out, for more means, into the ends of the earth.

II. But, *internally* the temple may be viewed for instruction and inspiration.

1. There was God's presence, for light and life and law. So is he with his house-builders now. But, was he with his people when the ark was with the Philistines? When under the foot of the captor sent to pun-

ish Israel for abuse of law and light and life? Let God's people be wise and study well the conditions of God's presence to aid and comfort, from Israel's history and the word of the gospel. When does the Carpenter's Son engage to fulfill the promise: "And, lo, I am with you alway, even unto the end of the world?"

2. There is the Priesthood with all their sacred offices. They had to be cleansed and anointed and sanctified. And for whom was this a model? Is not God's people at large a "royal priesthood?" What did the priest therein figure that the believer now is not required to do in reality? And the believer must be washed and anointed and consecrated by the regenerating and sanctifying power of the Holy Ghost. The Priest, without his preparation, was no more sacrilegious in going to the altar than is he who serves God without change of heart and life. "Holiness becometh thy house, oh Lord, forever." The command of the Carpenter's Son is: "Be ye perfect, even as your Father in heaven is perfect."

3. There was the High Priest and his atoning sacrifice before the Mercy Seat. This was annually repeated to show that we have perpetual need of the great atoning High Priest who has entered into the Holy of Holies and is making constant intercession. That intercession is sure for those whose faith is fixed on Him. For every duty, for every difficulty, for every trial, the law of success is, "looking unto Jesus."

4. The feasts of the Temple have their obviously corresponding duties in the Christian life, which must be observed. But, above all the Passover. That was

12

ever most prominently impressed under the old economy. This we keep by having the soul devoted to the great Redeemer by the ordinances of God's house, which should be the sacred privilege as well as the joyous duty of the believing heart. The state of heart which rejoices in Christ, our passover, is at the foundation of the Lord's house and its prosperous upbuilding.

5. The altar of incense suggests prayer, with which Solomon began to dedicate the Temple; and Solomon's blessings, with which the dedication was continued, suggest the Divine blessings implied in his manifest presence; and the vast sacrifices, with which the dedication was completed, suggest the sacrifices to which God's workmen are called and inspired by the great sacrifice of God's own Son—these and other parts and performances of the Temple are designed to impress valuable lessons on the minds and hearts of God's people.

6. But, I only refer further to the Courts of the Temple:

(1) There was a Court for God's people, whose duties and privileges have been considered.

(2) But, there was a Court for the Gentiles. This is a significant suggestion. Even exclusive Israel contemplated the heathen. Now the middle wall of partition is broken down. The world is the field for the gathering of material and builders for the Lord's house. Here is the grand obligation of the Church imposed by the Carpenter's Son: "Go ye into all the world and preach the gospel to every creature." It is only thus that God's promise to Abraham and Isaac

and Jacob and to his people of all ages can be realized, v'z: that in Christ all the nations of the earth shall be blessed.

III.—*What did the Temple represent?*

1. It represented the individual believer. Every part of the Temple should be in him ; for he is the Temple of the living God.

2. It represented the local Church. There was nothing in the Temple which should not have a counterpart in every Church of Christ. If the individual is a Temple of God, much more is a Church. In fact, it is by these myriads of personal temples and ecclesiastic temples, with all their duties and privileges, that the great Master-builder proposes to keep before our minds the great building comprehending all these miniature temples, as in the vast Cathedral many chapels may be found.

3. It represented the Church universal. There is a grand Church invisible, composed of the redeemed of all times and all climes, which have been gathering into the House of God since man fell and began to be redeemed. This House of God should inspire our individual and church services. The local Church is but the infant-school for training for the grander duties of those wider spheres of that family, a part of which is in heaven and a part on earth.

4. And did not the Temple represent a still broader house of God? Is there not to be a union of all things in heaven and in earth, in the dispensation of the fulness

of times, "in Christ?" Are there to be two houses of
God—one for the redeemed, the other for the angelic
host? Is there not to be the rebuilding of the universe
material and immaterial, and is not the whole to be the
great House of God? "In my Father's house are
many mansions"—many abodes in one house of the
Lord. That was the declaration of the Carpenter's
Son. With such representation of the Temple, what an
inspiration should the Temple be!

IV. *What of the representative Builders of the Temple?*

In general it may be said that it was to them a work
of love and of holy obedience, worthy of all their powers and resources, and to be conformed exactly to the
minute directions of God. Solomon said, "It is not a
house for man, but for God." Hence it must be according to God's plan and pattern alone.

1. See David. (1) See him in the matter of conformity to the Divine pattern. It is written: "Then
David gave to Solomon . . . the pattern of all that he
had by the spirit . . . of the house of the Lord. . . .
All this, said David, the Lord made me understand in
writing by his hand upon me, even all the works of this
pattern. And David said to Solomon his son, Be strong
and of good courage and do it." David entered upon
this work with full purpose of mind and heart, making
immense provision not only from the public treasury,
but munificent gifts of gold and silver from his own
purse—in his language, "of mine own proper goods."
He said, " I have set my affection unto the house of my

God." Hence, he gave himself, as he says, "mightily" to the work. And it was this example of David which stirred the hearts of the " princes," and " captains," and "fathers" and "people" of Israel to do likewise, when David cried out: "And who, then, is willing to conse- crate his service this day unto the Lord?" They brought into the treasury of the Lord's house their "precious stones," and their gold and silver, of the one more than "5000 talents" and of the other "10,000 talents," and 100,000 talents of iron. This was not strange, as David had made provision of material so great that it was "without number" and "without weight." "When the people rejoiced, for that they offered willingly, because with perfect heart they offered willingly to the Lord : and David the king also rejoiced with great joy." Nor was there the least self-adulation in these gifts to the Lord. David was humbled at the honor of thus being allowed to return to the Lord that which was the Lord's. "Blessed be the Lord," said he. " Thine, O Lord, is the great- ness, and the power, and the glory, and the victory and the majesty. . . . Both riches and honor come of thee, and thou reignest over all. . . . But who am I, and what is my people that we should be able to offer so willingly after this sort? for all things come of thee, and of thine own have we given thee. . . . Oh Lord our God, all this store that we have prepared to build thee a house for thine holy name cometh of thine hand, and is all thine own."

WHAT A STUDY THIS FOR GOD'S PEOPLE IN BUILD-
ING THE HOUSE OF THE LORD! *What a model for
their mind, their heart and their hands!*

2. See Solomon. He has been referred to as a representative worker of a practical kind upon the house of
the Lord: and so he was, and worthy is he of imitation
in his employment of wisdom, and wealth, and glory
and "largeness of heart" for the house of the Lord.
And none the less stimulating because he represented
the great Master-builder, who is the Supreme Model
for all his co-workers. Let us glance at Solomon, first,
as the symbol of the Carpenter's Son; and then as an
inspiring example for all.

(1) As the Symbol of the Carpenter's Son. Thus we
have viewed him before, but let us glance again, in
view of the scripture-records of his qualifications of
wealth, wisdom, glory and " largeness of heart."

(a) His wealth. An idea of his immense riches may
be obtained from the fact that, in addition to the wealth
which he inherited from his father, he had an annual
income of "666 talents of gold," not including the
income from business and commercial relations. From
every direction wealth was poured in upon him. It is
said of the Queen of Sheba that "she gave the king
a hundred and twenty talents of gold, and of spices
very great store, and precious stones: . . . And the
navy also of Hiram, that brought gold from Ophir,
brought in from Ophir great plenty of almug trees, and
precious stones." "And all the kings of Arabia, and
governors of the country," brought gold and silver to

Solomon. So abundant were his riches that it is written : "the king made silver in Jerusalem like stones." And this wealth he lavished most profusely upon the house of the Lord. Upon it and within it there seemed no further room for the bestowment of his silver and gold and precious stones; his cedar and his great hewn stones. Nothing could better represent consecration of the best gifts to God's service than Solomon's lavish expenditure on the House of the Lord.

(b) His wisdom. He desired this above wealth and honor, and God made him the wisest of men. His wisdom in government is seen in his judgment in the case of the two women and the child claimed by both ; his wisdom in theology, by his satisfaction of the Queen of Sheba, who came to prove him by hard questions "concerning the name of the Lord;" his wisdom, in building the Lord's house, by the sentiment, "who is able to build him a house, seeing the heaven and the heaven of heavens cannot contain him? Who am I, then, that I should build him a house, save only to burn sacrifice before him?" Of his wisdom we have this summary: "And Solomon's wisdom excelled the wisdom of all the children of the east country, and all the wisdom of Egypt. For he was wiser than all men : than Ethan the Ezrahite, and Heman and Chalcol and Darda, the sons of Mabol; and his fame was in all nations round about. And he spake three thousand proverbs ; and his songs were a thousand and five. And he spake of trees from the cedar tree that is in Lebanon even unto the hyssop that springeth out of the wall : he spake also of beasts and of fowl and of creeping things and of fishes. And there came of all people to hear the wisdom of Solomon from all kings of the earth, which had heard of his wisdom." And greater than his wisdom in botany and natural history, and literature and the sciences of divinity and political economy, was the practical wisdom of employing the best means and the best workmen for God's house. The most skilled artisans were imported, even those in whom God had given minds and hearts skilled pre-eminently for the work which they had to do. And all was done according to the pattern which David had received in writing of the Lord.

(c) Of his glory what shall be said? The glory of his court was such that it overwhelmed the wealthy monarch of the south, who brought large gifts, but who received of Solomon all her heart could desire. As to his fame it is written "All the earth sought to Solomon, to hear his wisdom, which God had put in his heart. And they brought every man his present, vessels of silver and vessels of gold, and garments and armor and spices and horses and mules, a rate year by year." "And Solomon reigned over all the kings from the river even unto the land of the Philistines and to the border of Egypt." And all this glory he used to give glory to the house of the Lord.

(d) But of his "largeness of heart:" Solomon's mind, went out grandly to the nations of the earth. The spread of his fame he associated with the spread of the name of God, saying of those of a far country that came to Jerusalem "for thy name's sake," that "they shall hear of thy great name and of thy strong hand and of thy stretched out arm :" and he prayed for the stranger, "Hear thou in heaven thy dwelling-place, and according to all that the stranger calleth to thee for : that all people of the earth may know thy name to fear thee as do thy people Israel; and that they may know that this house which I have builded is called by thy name." This was a heart broader than that of the Apostles before the day of Pentecost. But, it is written of Solomon, " And God gave him wisdom and understanding exceeding much, *and largeness of heart even as the sand that is on the sea shore.*" This was a heart equal to the taking in of the house of God, not only in its magnificent model, but in its universal reality !

Thus did this splendid royal mason well represent the more glorious Carpenter's Son, whose wisdom and power are the wisdom and power of God ; whose wealth is the earth's and the fulness thereof; and whose largeness of heart makes him the Friend of Sinners—the Saviour of the world ! And the Queen of Sheba's response to Solomon may well represent the world's reply to the world's great king : 2 Chron. ix. 8.

(2) But Solomon was not only a symbol, he was an inspiration for all the Lord's builders in all time— especially for those who are most able to " lend a helping hand." Solomon did not hesitate to call on a wealthy king to aid in this work, and Hiram, king of Tyre, when thus called on, blessed God that he had raised up a wise Son to David to build a great house

unto the praise of God. And shall any man think himself too great, too wise, too rich, too famous, too broad-minded and broad-hearted to put his hand to God's house? Let him stand rebuked before Hiram, King of Tyre; let him be covered with shame in the presence of King Solomon! Rather, let him be cast to the earth, and cover his lips in the dust, in the presence of the King of Kings and Lord of Lords, the Lord God Almighty, who, because the builder of God's house, came to earth as "the Carpenter's Son."

V. *The Dedication.*

Grand was the prayer of Solomon, and his blessing upon the people, surrounded by the immense multitudes, of whom 150,000 were strangers from other lands. But, the grandest of all of the Dedication was, as has been said, the stupendous sacrifice of 22,000 oxen, and 120,000 sheep! To human eyes that was merely awful: to the eyes of faith, seeing its representation of God's great sacrifice for which the house was built, it was awfully sublime! And God came down in fire: and the glory of the Lord filled the house! The prayer of Saints and the sacrifice of the Lamb of God will ever secure the Divine presence among his people engaged in the construction of the house of "the Carpenter's Son."

I only add that the Temple's erection was the third pivotal period of the ante-Christian world's history, of which the two others were the Tabernacle and the Ark.

CHAPTER XXI.

IN CAPTIVITY: REBUILDING TEMPLE.

The Lord is Governor among the nations.—Ps. xxii. 28.

THE destruction of Jerusalem and the captivity of God's people taught the great lesson that God's service and God's people are not mere names; that sin is sin, and to be punished, wherever found; and that "in every nation he that feareth him and worketh righteousness is accepted by him." In the distant past this last principle had had signal illustrations. The Hebrew thought that the divine presence and power for good was only to be manifested to the elected people, separated by their genealogy, their rites and their traditions from the rest of the world. But God had appeared graciously among those unknown to Jewish extraction or to the covenants of Israel. Who was Jethro, the priest of Midian? and yet he wisely and divinely instructed the law-giver of Israel. Who was Melchisedec, the king of Salem? yet he was the God-ordered type of the personal priesthood of the Lord. Job does not appear in the genealogy of the children of Abraham, and yet he is divinely recorded "a man perfect and upright, and one that feared God and eschewed evil;" and is celebrated in the Hebrew Scriptures as one of the three holiest men of the world's history. And has he not given to mankind, in his incomparable historic drama, which is full of divine

187

truth, one of the grandest expositions of the unsearcha-
bleness, almightiness, and absolute independence of
him who sitteth upon the throne of the universe, doing
his own pleasure in the armies of heaven and among
the inhabitants of the earth, so that none can stay his
arm or say, What doest thou? And was it not an
indication of God's care for the nations that the Hebrews
were taken in infancy and reared into a nation among
pagans, which, by the way, was a type of "the Carpenter's Son," of whom it is recorded, "Out of Egypt
have I called my Son." And as to Israel's relation to
Egypt, was there ever a grander demonstration of divine
sovereignty than the slave-son of Jacob becoming the
virtual head of this mighty empire, and his family, who
came as beggars into the land, going out the miraculous
conquerors of Pharaoh and his hosts? Among their
masters of the Babylonish captivity, to whom reference
has been made, other blocks of truth were embedded
for the foundation of the Lord's Temple. Divine
Providence, threading the complications of court in-
trigues and corruptions in the days of Esther—a Hebrew
captive wonderfully made the queen of Persia—published her God's omniscience and omnipotence and omnipresence by the marvellous preservation of his people
and the destruction of their enemies, all by royal decree,
not only in Shusan (the palace of Ahasuerus), but
throughout his realm of one hundred and twenty-seven
provinces, stretching from India to Ethiopia. The fact
of this all-pervading divine providence, which is another
name for the presence of Jehovah, was celebrated by a

perpetual feast, called Purim, and by court records of the decrees of Esther and Mordecai.   It was worth the captivity of a nation to have the name of their living and true God so exalted among the heathen by the providence that exalted his faithful servants, as implied in this record: "Then Esther the queen, the daughter of Abihail and Mordecai the Jew, wrote with all authority . . . and the decree of Esther confirmed the matters of Purim; and it was written in the book . . . And all the acts of his power and might, and the declaration of the greatness of Mordecai, wherein the king advanced him, are they not written in the book of the chronicles of the kings of Media and Persia?"   In the eventful reigns of several monarchs in the land of the captivity, how Jehovah-glorifying were the divine wonders.   For instance—the divinely given interpretations and revelations of Daniel; and the sublime moral courage of the three Hebrew captive youths, who defied to his face the powerful despot, who would force them, by the sanctions of the fiery furnace, to idolatrous blasphemy of their God, thus: "O Nebuchadnezzar, we are not careful to answer thee in this matter.   If it be so, our God whom we serve is able to deliver us from the burning fiery furnace, and he will deliver us out of thine hand, O king.   But if not, be it known unto thee, O king, that we will not serve thy gods, nor worship the golden image which thou hast set up."   What a victory for their God, was the decree of the monarch, after seeing "the Son of God" and his preserving power—two great foundation truths—in the midst of the flames: "Therefore I make a decree, that every people, nation and language which speak anything amiss against the God of Shadrach, Meshach and Abednego, shall be cut in pieces . . . because there is no other God that can deliver after this sort." And personally humbled by the God of his captives, he confesses: "Now I, Nebuchadnezzar, praise and extol and honor the King of heaven, all whose works are truth, and his ways judgment." A great foundation truth of the captivity was that little stone, cut out of the rock without hands, which demolished the grand image and filled the whole earth! But the most marvellous and glorifying revelation of the God of Israel, was the rebuilding of the Temple of Jerusalem, through the agency of Ezra and Nehemiah, at the expense of the royal treasuries, by Cyrus and Artaxerxes! Watching the erection of the Lord's house how profoundly must these pagan monarchs have been impressed. These two men, Ezra and Nehemiah, were themselves a grand revelation. The intense godliness of the one and the magnificent nobility of the other proclaimed aloud the truth and the God of Israel. Ezra warns off polluting hands from God's house, replying to Sanballat and Tobiah: "Ye have nothing to do with us to build a house to our God;" and overwhelmed by his people's sins, this holy priest makes anguished confession, as if personally involved in the transgression, reminding of Moses, who would make himself an atonement for the people, and of Paul, who, for his brethren, could wish himself accursed from Christ. Into the noble character of Nehemiah, which must have been observed in the Persian court, a glimpse is given by two little incidents. First, Discovering that the grandson of the high priest was son-in-law to Sanballat, the Horonite, he says: "I chased him away from me." Second, When advised to save his life by fleeing into the temple, he replied: "Should such a man as I flee? and who is there that being as I am would go into the temple to save his life? I will not go in." And with fine political and moral insight into his adviser he adds: "He was hired that I should be afraid and do so, and sin, and that they might have matter for an evil report, that they might reproach me." His adviser had been hired by Sanballat, whose daughter's husband, Nehemiah had *chased out of his sight!* David describes the man to abide in the Lord's presence as one "in whose eyes a vile person is contemned." The books of Ezra and Nehemiah are replete with pictures of the godliness and the goodliness of these two builders of God's house. But to royal pagan eyes, marvellous must have been the complete subordination of all the affairs of Jerusalem, municipal, political, social, and international, to the single work of erecting a Temple, which in heathen nations is only a subordinate concern. Jerusalem is for the Temple, not the Temple for Jerusalem. This is a new, a divine idea, illustrated practically in their absorption, during their national restoration, in the law, the Psalms, the Covenants, the holiness, the erection of God's house. How different from heathen nationality! There was no fanaticism. City walls were necessary for the Temple's safety, and houses were needed for worshippers in the Temple; and "the people had a mind to work," and work they did upon their homes, and the defences of the city, with trowel in one hand and sword in the other: but the Temple—the Temple of God—was the end of their labors and hopes.   They recalled the taunt as they hung their harps on the willows by the rivers of Babylon, "Sing us one of the songs of Zion," and their mournful reply: "How shall we sing the Lord's song in a strange land?"   And they longed to sing it again in the courts of their God.

"And when the builders laid the foundation of the temple of the Lord, they set the priests in their apparel with trumpets, and the Levites, the sons of Asaph, with cymbals, to praise the Lord after the ordinance of David, King of Israel.   And they sang together by course, in praising and giving thanks unto the Lord; because he is good, for his mercy endureth forever toward Israel.   And all the people shouted with a great shout when they praised the Lord, because the foundation of the house of the Lord was laid.   But many of the priests, and the Levites, and chief of the fathers who were ancient men that had seen the first house, when the foundation of this house was laid before their eyes, wept with a loud voice, and many shouted aloud for joy: So that the people could not discern the noise of the shout of joy from the noise of the weeping of the people: for the people shouted with a loud shout and the noise was heard afar off."

The Sabbath of this theocratic civilization must have

been very suggestive to these befriending and God-inspired monarchs of the east. The following record by Nehemiah may have been read in the court of Persia, and might well be read in the courts and offices of all governments seeking the best interests of their people: "In those days saw I in Judah some treading wine-presses on the Sabbath, and bringing in sheaves, and leading asses: as also wine grapes and figs and all manner of burdens which they brought into Jerusalem on the Sabbath day, and I testified against them in the day wherein they sold victuals. There dwelt men of Tyre also therein, which brought fish and all manner of ware, and sold on the Sabbath, unto the children of Judah and in Jerusalem. Then I contended with the nobles of Judah and said unto them, What evil thing is this that ye do and profane the Sabbath day? Did not your fathers thus, and did not our God bring all this evil upon us, and upon this city? yet ye bring more wrath upon Israel by profaning the Sabbath. And it came to pass that when the gates of Jerusalem began to be dark before the Sabbath, I commanded that the gates should be shut, and charged that they should not be opened till after the Sabbath : and some of my servants set I at the gates that there should no burden be brought in on the Sabbath day. So the merchants and sellers of all kind of ware lodged without Jerusalem once or twice. Then I testified against them, and said unto them, Why lodge ye about the wall? if ye do so again I will lay hands on you. From that time forth came they no more on the Sabbath. And I commanded the

13

Levites, that they should cleanse themselves and that they should come and keep the gates to sanctify the Sabbath day. Remember me, O my God, concerning this also, and spare me according to the greatness of thy mercy."

And who can say that these foundation truths, imbedded in the distant orient, did not lead to Jerusalem, at the birth of "the Carpenter's Son," the wise men of the east? How strange that these wise men are called kings: and that their remains are enshrined—" as they say "—in one of the grand temples of the Christian world. The Temple of Jerusalem was built by God; and, the God-building idea engrafted in the human mind, likes to fancy, at times, that other of the world's grandest edifices have had the same origin. The pyramids are said, by an architect who has devoted many years to the study of the Ark and the Temple of Solomon, to have been built by the author of these structures, by the hand of the builder of the former structure. The same idea is half seriously presented, with regard to the grand Cathedral covering the shrine of the three Christ-seeking kings of the east, in a letter by the wife of the author of Ben-Hur (published in the *Richmond Dispatch*, July 15, 1888, and copied here, by permission of its editor), perchance to elevate the mind to the glory of the Temple of Jerusalem and of that greater temple, of which the Cathedral at Cologne and that Temple of Jerusalem are only faint shadows and symbols.

"How well I remember that day—that golden day—at Cologne ! The print of the Roman yoke is on it yet, for the Church of St. Marie holds the site of the Roman Capitol, and has resounded with the armed tread of the Legions of Trajan.

"Of the treasures of the Cathedral nothing compares with the shrine of the Magi, the tomb behind the grand altar, where Gothic windows cast varied lights on the tessellated pavement and along the Ionic pillars. The casket is six feet long, modelled as a Roman Basilica, enriched with artistic, sacred figures, carved jewels, and chased and enamelled ornamentation. . . .

"The carved stones belong to classic antique art, and the lapidary's work is delicate and marvellously fine. At the head end of the shrine is a movable panel which the keeper slips aside, and behold! three bare skulls, each circled with a diamond crown.

"The names are in square letters set with rubies which flash like flame:

GASPAR. MELCHIOR. BALTHAZAR.

". . . We lingered about the shrine as became believing pilgrims; we marked the scene of the baptism of Jesus in the river Jordan, the panel representing the Redeemer seated on His throne, with his right hand raised and holding the Book of Life in his left; the Virgin and Child, carved by some devout worker, who prayed as he wrought and was blessed in his labors. It is the finest specimen of mediæval art, and is fitly placed in the first of sanctuaries. Not strange that the making of such a structure is cloudy with myths and traditions. There are the pictured windows of world-wide fame. Oh, it is a pity to die without seeing them. They were clear glass once; angels brushed them with their wings, and lo! they took on many-colored radiance like sunset dyes. Ethereal hands finished them in a single night, and vainly does mortal artist try to copy tints which were never spread on earthly palette.

"And no one knows who designed the famous cathedral. The legend-haunted Rhine abounds in explanation of the matchless work. . . .

"I like best to think it was conceived in the valley of vision under some divine inspiration. Better to me the tale that an emperor, generous and munificent, long ago summoned his builders together and promised them eternal fame if they would build a fane which should surpass all other fanes. There should be no limit in design, no bound to expense, no question as to time. Said the monarch to the artisans on bended knees before him : 'Let its splendor be like the first temple on Mt. Moriah. What I ask is perfection.' . . .

"At the appointed day, plans and models were brought, drawings and traceries laid at the foot of the throne. But as one after another was unrolled the proud Emperor said: 'They will not do; this cathedral is to keep my name in remembrance while the world remains to let its spires point upward.' The designers left the presence chamber, their eyes full of rage and tears of disappointment. 'Who but the devil can satisfy a king who asks impossibilities?' said they. One workman lingered behind when the train of aspirants had departed. He had no roll or parchment or box of models;

he was an old man, bent and weak, wearing a green coat and a gray cap.

" 'Grant me this favor, O King,' he demanded in a shrill, piping voice, ' one day more to work at my draw-ings. I am so near to my ideal, so near. I have sought it through prayers and fastings; and last night I almost touched the plan, the design of a temple which shall eclipse the splendor of others as the sun outshines the small stars. My meditations are nearly ended, but the picture I see with the eye of my soul will not yet shape itself to my hand. It is very near.' He unrolled a slight parchment from his bosom. 'Dost thou see aught, O Emperor, a shape of beauty on this scroll?'

" 'I see nothing,' said the monarch, coldly; 'its blank page has no lines for my sight.'

"The little old man groaned in anguish and trembled. His hand shook as he refolded the paper.

" 'It is as I feared; the pencil of light was but a snare and deceit. Only grant one day more, O most merciful, and if I fail let me go back to my cell, for I have taken holy orders, and I will spend the few days left of threescore and ten in repentance that I let ambi-tion under my cowl.'

"The pious Emperor graciously spoke : 'One day more, holy man, I give you ; and in your prayers forget not the name of your sovereign, who is low as the meanest in the sight of our common Master.'

"Then the old man kissed the royal hand held out to him and backed like a courtier out of the chamber.

"The monk was devout and humble. ' What am I,

that I should win a great name?' he asked of himself;
'yet the shepherd on the plain of Midian was no more
than the monk vowed to perpetual poverty, resting his
naked feet on the bare floor of the cloister. 'O Blessed
Virgin, O Holy Mary,' he prayed, 'help the weakest
of thy children, for my spirit fainteth.'

"The pale outline of a superb temple floated in the
air about him. He snatched his pencil and unrolled his
paper, but the vague, formless thing faded like a dis-
solving view—the dizzy pinnacles floated away.

"Overcome with the long mental strain, he burst
into tears of despair, and exclaimed: 'Into thy hands,
O Mary, I leave it!' So a sweet peace descended on
him like a dove. He sunk to sleep in his oaken chair,
and at the mystic hour of midnight, when the veil
between the two worlds, seen and unseen, grows dim, he
was roused by an awakening light.

"It was not like the sun, nor yet of the moon;
neither was it a lamp nor the light of tapers. Awe-
struck and enraptured, he sat still while his cell filled
with the heavenly radiance. His eyes gradually became used to the shining wonder, and he was aware of
the presence of four men with starry crowns on their
heads.

"The first was a grave man, with venerable white
beard covering his breast; in his hand he held a pair of
compasses. The second, more youthful in appearance,
carried a mason's square. The third, a strong man
with heavy curling beard, held a rule; and the fourth,
a handsome lad with light, flowing auburn locks, brought

a level, thus betokening they were masters of the sacred art of Freemasonry. They glided in with solemn, soundless tread, and with them, last to come into his dazzled sight, entered the saintly Virgin, clothed with celestial beauty, carrying in her right hand a lily with silver-white flowers.

"'I have heard thy prayer, and am here to help thee in thy need,' said the Virgin to the awe-stricken architect. 'One penalty I lay upon thee.'

"'What is it, O Queen of Heaven?'

"'For worldly ambition, and because thou hast said in thy heart, 'Solomon, I will surpass thee,' thy name shall be forgotten among the sons of men.'

"'But,' cried the disappointed artisan, 'it is in hope of fame I have toiled, prayed, suffered. I have out-watched Orion and the sun has looked down on me as it rose. The cathedral of my heart and soul is to be the monument which he who sees will ask in wonder and amaze, Who was the architect?'

"'There is but one condition,' said Mary, mildly; 'choose this instant, the hour passes.'

"He covered his face with his hands and wept aloud; a few moments his sobs echoed through the cell and the struggle was passed. He raised his eyes to the Blessed Virgin in thankfulness and exclaimed: 'If only my holy work lives on, I am content that my name is written in Heaven.'

"'I shall write it with my own hand in the Book of Remembrance, where the prayers of the saints are recorded, for thou art worthy,' said the tender voice.

'In six centuries, as men count time, the cathedral will be finished, hallowed by the prayers of such disciples as thou, and radiant with angelic light.'

"She made a sign of command to the master-masons, and they sketched with rapid touches a design which shone like fire on the bare walls of the cell. The forest of stone pillars shot on high, the arches curved to meet them, and two majestic towers, flying butresses and pinnacles, went up higher and higher, like winged things, into the blue of heaven. In silence the old monk (I grieve that his name is lost) contemplated the divine revelation. When the gray light of dawn stole into his cell the vision softly faded, but the plans drawn by the four masters of the art of architecture under the eye of the Virgin Mother were burned into his memory. The cool breeze of morning fanned his forehead, and the sun cheerily looked into his narrow window. It was not the fever of a madman nor the delusion of Satan. He rose and whispered, 'When I wash my forehead with fresh dew the mists will clear away.' He went into the garden and walked an hour, all the while in prayer. He returned to his cell and spread the untouched parchment. An invisible force guided his hand swiftly as light travels. Ground plan and elevation, longitudinal and transverse sections, delicate detail drawings were made before noon, and when the minster clock struck twelve the happy architect laid his perfected sketch at the foot of the throne.

"But such a work—firm as adamant, light as lace, lovely as music—is not complete in one, two or three generations, and after exhausting wars the masons were dismissed by the government.   Then at night the ghost of the architect would walk the walls, moaning, like the winds in the pines : ' I cannot rest till this work goes on ; my bed is hard.   It is no place of rest till the men come back to their sheds.'   He was always dressed in green (for the German ghosts are not sworn to white robes), with a gray cap on his head, a measuring-rod and a pair of compasses in his hand.

" Not till the times of the good Emperor William was the final wreath of stone foliage laid in place, just 632 years to a day after the laying of the first foundation.

" And thus was created the fairest temple outside of the City of Precious Stones.   Fit resting place for the shrines of the Wise Men from the East—

"THE THREE KINGS OF COLOGNE."

Bright is this picture of the fane that rises above the mythical tomb of the three kings, as the grander Cathedral of Rome rises above the equally mythical tomb of the Apostle Peter.   But bright as is the picture, it is only as the dawn is to midday in comparison with the reality of that Temple going up by the prayers and labors of saints to the honor of the King of saints, which is " exceeding magnifical of glory," and is dedicated to the life and death and ascension of him to whom the wise men of the east brought their offerings of " gold and frankincense and myrrh," and who is indeed " the King eternal, immortal, invisible, the only wise God, to whom be honor and glory for ever and ever.   *Amen.*"

CHAPTER XXII.

IN THE PROPHETS.

For the testimony of Jesus is the spirit of prophecy.—Rev. xix. 10.

THE Carpenter's Son said: "Search the Scriptures, for in them ye think ye have life, and they are they that testify of me." We have seen how they testify of his presence and power in every age of the world, and of the origin and progress and completion of the house he was anointed to erect. He himself reviewed the Scriptures, in this respect, before some of his fellow-workmen. The record is: "And beginning at Moses and all the prophets, he expounded unto them in all the Scriptures the things concerning himself." And in that day of his incarnation he predicted things of himself, which are written in the New Testament, and have come to pass. Need we refer to his predictions of his own death and resurrection and ascension, and his coming again on the day of Pentecost, and his abiding with his people who go forth to build his house among the nations of the earth? And, in his Apocalypse, what striking pictures of his works, already accomplished and to be achieved, even unto the completion of the Lord's house. And as he is the beginning and ending of all revelation, all these predictions of holy writ are from him. It was he that foretold of Israel's blessings, should they obey the Lord, and of their cursings when

202

they rebelled against his commandments. It was he that predicted what should befall the nations in the day of Israel; and what shall come to pass, with regard to his people and with regard to the world, even unto the end of time. And plainly has he foretold with regard to himself, in connection with the building of God's house, from the very beginning. His mouthpiece was often the prophets, but he was the spirit of their prophecy. Hear the words of Peter, with regard to the great salvation, "Of which salvation the prophets have inquired and searched diligently, who prophesied of the grace that should come unto you: searching what or what manner of time *the Spirit of Christ which was in them* did signify, when it testified aforehand the sufferings of Christ and the glory that should follow, . . . which things the angels desire to look into." And all through their writings, the writers of the great salvation quote the words of ancient prophecy with regard to the Carpenter's Son, which he himself predicted. As a single example, his first biographer, Matthew, quotes, in his first two chapters, no less than four passages of the ancient prophets, with regard to this Son of David and Abraham, the Carpenter's Son.

And what were some of his ancient predictions with regard to himself? In his own person, he predicted, to Satan himself, that he would be his opposing power in the world's history, in the striking words: "And I will put enmity between thee and the woman, and between thy seed and her seed: it shall bruise thy head and thou shalt bruise his heel." And has not this come to

pass? And how fully the triumph of the woman's
seed over "the old serpent, which is the devil," shall
come to pass, was predicted through Abraham and Isaac
and Jacob, in their prophecy, that in their "seed," which
Paul says is "Christ," all the nations of the earth shall
be blessed. And through the dying Jacob the Lord
God reported prophetically progress in this great triumph, when he declared, "The sceptre shall not depart
from Judah, nor a lawgiver from between his feet, until
Shiloh come: and unto him shall the gathering of the
people be." And did not Judah stand until the Carpenter's Son, the Lawgiver and King of Israel, came?
By the mouth of Baalam even, he repeats, "There
shall come a star out of Jacob and a sceptre shall rise
out of Israel, . . . out of Jacob shall come he that
shall have dominion." And is not this the Prophet
and Lawgiver predicted by Moses, "And the Lord said
unto me, . . . I will raise them up a Prophet from
among their brethren, like unto thee, and will put my
words in his mouth"? Hence are Moses and the Carpenter's Son coupled in the gospel thus: "The law
came by Moses, but grace and truth by Jesus Christ."
Even in the remotest times of recorded history, we hear
him speaking in the Patriarch of Uz, "For I know that
my Redeemer liveth, and that he shall stand at the
latter day upon the earth: And though after my skin
worms destroy this body, yet in my flesh shall I see
God." David is a favorite mouthpiece, and through
him the Holy One of Israel anticipates his anguish on
Calvary, crying, "My God, my God, why hast thou

forsaken me!" And describes himself, "My strength is dried up like a potsherd; and my tongue cleaveth to my jaws; and thou hast brought me into the dust of death." And even of his heartless murderers he predicts, "They look and stare upon me. They part my garments among them, and cast lots upon my vesture." Through the Evangelical Prophet, Isaiah, he gives in advance the salient points of his whole earthly history, as the Carpenter's Son, from his miraculous birth and divine appellations, through all his sufferings and injuries for the sake of the sinner, even unto his death and burial and ascension to glory; and gives it so vividly that the picture is a perfect portrait of the original, which proves him present with the prophet and proves the prophecy the word of God. Though depicted seven hundred years before the birth of Mary's son, the picture seems painted after his death. He himself, in the days of his flesh, reads from Isaiah the passage: "The Spirit of the Lord is upon me because he hath anointed me to preach the gospel to the poor," and declares that it was fulfilled in his mission; and the evangelist Philip, taking as his text the passage from this prophet, "He was led as a sheep to the slaughter," preached unto the Ethiopian, "JESUS." Jerome said that Isaiah's scripture was not a prophecy, but a *gospel*. And does not Cyrus, whom the prophet called by name as the coming builder of the Lord's house, which Josephus says was the cause of that monarch's rebuilding the Temple of Jerusalem, appear like a type of Christ — the Master-builder of that more splendid and enduring

Temple whose glory this seer of God saw in enwrapped visions? Without regard to chronological order, I remark, with respect to the great inspirer of prophetical truth, that his voice is plainly heard through *Malachi:* "Remember ye the law of Moses, my servant, which I commanded unto him in Horeb for all Israel, with the statutes and judgments . . . Bring ye all the tithes into the storehouse and prove me if I will not pour you out a blessing that there shall not be room enough to receive it . . . Behold I will send my messenger and he shall prepare the way before me; and the Lord, whom ye seek, shall suddenly come to his temple, even the messenger of the covenant whom ye delight in . . . But who shall abide the day of his coming? . . . Behold I will send you Elijah the prophet, before the coming of the great and dreadful day of the Lord: and he shall turn the heart of the fathers to the children, and the heart of the children to their fathers, lest I come and smite the earth with a curse . . . But unto you that fear his name shall the Sun of righteousness arise with healing in his wings . . . And all nations shall call you blessed. . . . For from the rising of the sun even unto the going down of the same, my name shall be great among the Gentiles. . . . And they shall be mine, saith the Lord of hosts, in that day when I make up my jewels; and I will spare them as a man spareth his own son that serveth him." Who speaks thus by the mouth of *Zechariah:* "I will return to Jerusalem with mercies: my house shall be built in it . . . behold I will bring forth my servant the BRANCH. For, behold, the stone that I have laid before Joshua; upon one stone shall be seven eyes . . . Behold the man whose name is THE BRANCH: and he shall grow up out of his place, and he shall build the temple of the Lord . . . Rejoice greatly, O daughter of Zion; shout, O daughter of Jerusalem: behold, thy King cometh unto thee: he is just and having salvation; lowly, and riding upon an ass, and upon a colt the foal of an ass . . . Awake, O sword, against my Shepherd, and against the man that is my fellow, saith the Lord of hosts: smite the Shepherd, and the sheep shall be scattered: and I will turn my hand upon the little ones . . . In that day shall there be upon the bells of the horses, HOLINESS UNTO THE LORD."

By *Haggai* he says: "Build the house and I will take pleasure in it. . . . I will shake all nations, and the Desire of all nations shall come: and I will fill this house with glory . . . The silver is mine, and the gold is mine, saith the Lord of hosts. The glory of this latter house shall be greater than the former: and in this place will I give peace, saith the Lord of hosts." Sad are his words through *Zephaniah;* but he speaks comfortingly of the distant future: "I will make you a name and a praise among all people of the earth, when I turn back your captivity before your eyes, saith the Lord." Through the lips of *Habakkuk*, he denounces woe, woe, woe against the sins of his people, and against their terrible enemies; but he puts his Spirit in the heart of the prophet, who utters this beautiful language of faith: "Although the fig tree shall not blossom, neither shall fruit be in the vines; the labour of the olive shall fail, and the fields shall yield no meat; the flock shall be cut off from the fold, and there shall be no herd in the stalls: yet I will rejoice in the Lord, I will joy in the God of my salvation. The Lord God is my strength, and he will make my feet like hinds' feet and he will make me to walk upon mine high places." Woes are poured forth against Nineveh, through the prophet *Nahum*; but the Lord saith to his people: "Though I have afflicted thee, I will afflict thee no more . . . Behold upon the mountains the feet of him that bringeth good tidings, that publisheth peace!" By the prophetic Spirit of the Lord, *Micah* predicts that out of Bethlehem shall come forth a "ruler in Israel whose goings forth have been from everlasting . . . and whose name shall be great unto the ends of the earth. . . . In the last days it shall come to pass that the mountain of the house of the Lord shall be established in the top of the mountain, and many nations shall come and say, Come, and let us go up to the mountain of the Lord, and to the house of the God of Jacob.' *Jonah* was an unworthy prophet, but he typified the buried Lord, and in the whale's belly glorified him by looking unto his "holy temple," and confessing: "Salvation is of the Lord." Only the Lord of all could utter these words through *Obadiah:* "Behold, I have made thee small among the heathen . . . but the kingdom shall be the Lord's." Terrible are the divine words by the herdman of Tekoa, *Amos;* but the Lord is gracious, saying: "Can two walk together except they be agreed? . . . Seek ye me, and live. Seek not Bethel, nor enter into Gilgal. . . . Seek the Lord and ye shall live. Seek him that maketh the seven stars and Orion, and turneth the shadow of death into the morning. . . . It is he that buildeth his stories in the heaven; . . . The Lord is his name. . . . In that day will I raise up the tabernacle of David that is fallen . . . and I will build it as in the day of old." The Spirit and the times of refreshing from above, promised by the Carpenter's Son, was predicted by his Spirit in the prophet *Joel:* "I will pour out my Spirit upon all flesh; and your sons and your daughters shall prophesy, your old men shall dream dreams, your young men shall see visions . . . and it shall come to pass that whosoever shall call upon the name of the Lord shall be saved." Whose words are these by the mouth of *Hosea:* "The Holy One is in the midst of thee . . . I will ransom thee from the fear of the grave: I will redeem thee from death. Oh, death, I will be thy plagues; oh, grave, I will be thy destruction! . . . Take with thee words and turn to the Lord; say unto him, Take away all iniquity, and receive us graciously: so will we render the calves of our lips; . . . I will heal their backsliding, I will love them freely; . . . I will be as the dew unto Israel; he shall grow as the lily, and cast his roots as Lebanon. Who is wise, and he shall understand these things? . . . for the ways of the Lord are right, and the just shall walk in them." And what shall be said of the Lord of inspiration in the heart and on the lips of the greater prophets, *Daniel,* and *Jeremiah,* and *Ezekiel?* Most manifestly was he

14

with the hero of the lions' den and the wisest man of
the courts of the east, as history has already demon-
strated; and it was not strange that the exact time
of his personal advent and sacrifice, predicted by this
man, who is recorded by holy writ as one of the three
holiest of the sons of men, should occur as indicated in
confirmation of the covenant of the Godhead. As to
Jeremiah and Ezekiel, they were possessed of the Master's Spirit of prophecy under very diverse circumstances
—the one remaining amid the desolation of ruined Jerusalem, the other going captive to the land of the Chal-
deans. It is not strange that the Carpenter's Son was
thought by some to be the prophet Jeremiah, so like was
"the man of sorrows" to the suffering and weeping
prophet, who suffered in person indignity, injustice,
cruelty and martyrdom; and whose lamentations over
the sins and ruin of his people, depicted in the most
graphic and heart-rending manner, are only exceeded
by the soul-wail of him who cried, "my soul is exceed-
ingly sorrowful, even unto death," over the world's sin
and overthrow, which was the unutterable anguish of
this vicarious and atoning sufferer. How like the Master's rebukes and pathos these words of the prophet:
"Trust ye not in lying words, saying, The temple of
the Lord, the temple of the Lord, the temple of the
Lord are these. . . . Is this house, which is called by
my name, become a den of robbers in your eyes? Behold, even I have seen it, saith the Lord. . . . O Jerusalem, wash thine heart from wickedness, that thou
mayest be saved! . . . And I will give you pastors

according to mine heart, which shall feed you with knowledge and understanding . . . For these things I weep; mine eye, mine eye runneth down with water, because the Comforter that should relieve my soul is far from me; my children are desolate, because the enemy prevailed. . . . Mine eye runneth down with rivers of water for the destruction of the daughter of my people!" Jeremiah's prophecy is the utterance of the very spirit of the agonies of Gethsemane and Calvary. Ezekiel had a face of "flint" and a forehead of "adamant," and his utterances were as powerful and terrific as they were magnificent and mysterious. Away from Jerusalem, the Temple was more constantly and more vividly before his mind, and his superlatively grand visions on the bank of the Chebar were derived, by inspiration, mainly from the Temple. And most worthy of note is it that one-sixth of all his prophetic scripture is given to a minute and exalted picture of the Temple to be erected, which was not realized in the Temple of Jerusalem. He had belabored his people for building the Lord's house with "untempered mortar;" for defiling it by false and wicked worship. And so terrible was the wickedness of the land, that he declares and reiterates that the presence in it of even Noah, Daniel and Job could not save it! But by the Word and the Spirit the dry bones of the valley are clothed with flesh and filled with life and stand up, "an exceeding great army." This is to overthrow the adversaries of God and his temple. Thus is there to be a resurrection of the dead world, under the power of him who is "the resurrection and the life," and all nations shall be gathered into the house and city of the Lord. In the vision of this temple, depicted so particularly by the prophet, the Lord said : " The uncircumcised in heart shall not enter my sanctuary: . . . I will give them a new heart." And he called the temple " The place of my throne and the place of the soles of my feet, where I will dwell in the midst of the children of Israel forever;" and the name of the city surrounding it is, "The Lord is there." What temple is that? Is it any other than that of the New Jerusalem—the city of our God ?

But, midway between the old and the new dispensations, stood the greatest of the prophets,—that Elijah-like man of the desert, whose rugged mien and coarse food and severe raiment were in rigid harmony with his robust spirit and powerful voice,—whose mission was represented as " the voice of one crying in the wilderness ;" that preacher of fruitful repentance, and of baptism unto faith in him who was to baptize in the Holy Ghost and in fire; who emptied cities and districts by the attractive power of his terrible eloquence; of whom Matthew wrote, " Then went out to him Jerusalem and all Judea and all the region round about Jordan, and were baptized of him, confessing their sins ;" and one greater than Matthew said: "Among those that are born of women there is not a greater prophet than *John the Baptist* "—that man on whom great honor was conferred by a bloody martyrdom for the truth, and the greatest honor conferred on mortal man, as witnessed in this record :

"Then cometh Jesus from Galilee to Jordan unto John, to be baptized of him. But John forbade him, saying, I have need to be baptized of thee, and comest thou to me? And Jesus answering said unto him, Suffer it to be so now: for thus it becometh us to fulfil all righteousness. Then he suffered him. And Jesus, when he was baptized, went up straightway out of the water: and, lo, the heavens were opened unto him, and he saw the Spirit of God descending like a dove, and lighting upon him: and, lo, a voice from heaven, saying, This is my beloved Son, in whom I am well pleased." That grand man came, not only as the immediate herald of him whose shoe-latchet he was unworthy to loose, but as the mouthpiece of the Spirit of the "Holy One of Israel." Though his cousin after the flesh, he did not know him, in his true nature and work, until he was revealed by the Spirit and the dove in the baptismal waters. When beclouded in mind, by the horrid dungeon of Herod's Castle, he sends for light to him who replies, as conclusive testimony of his Messiahship, "The poor have the gospel preached unto them." Thus this mighty man of God, inspired by the same Spirit that inspired all the prophets of God, looking back into the long past, through the sacrificial ritual of the Temple and Tabernacle, and back to the altars of the first inhabitants of our earth visited by the manifested Son of God, and yet back to the "Lamb slain from the foundation of the world;" and doubtless looking forward to the end of all this symbolic blood, in a greater, all-comprehending, sacrificial offering for the world's restoration, coming directly upon "the Carpenter's Son," whom he had baptized, and in the presence of the people, before whom the world-moving John was to decrease, and the "Son of Mary" to increase, cried: "Behold, the Lamb of God!"—the Lamb of God that taketh away the sin of the world; the Lamb for whose offering our globe was built as an altar, and for whose glory is erecting, by the combined creatures of his hand, the Temple universal and eternal, whose foundations are cemented in the blood of this Lamb of God. The Alpha and Omega of all prophecy and all revelation and all the universe is "the Carpenter's Son."

CHAPTER XXIII.

IN THE GOSPEL.

I am Alpha and Omega, the beginning and the ending, saith the Lord.
—Rev. i. 8.

THAT was a striking and suggestive scene when "the Carpenter's Son," who was born "in the city of David," and of whom the angel Gabriel said, before his birth, "The Lord God shall give unto him the throne of his father David, and he shall reign over the house of Jacob forever," and whom the godly Simeon, when the child, eight days old, was brought into the temple to receive the seal of the Covenant with Abraham, called "A light to lighten the gentiles and the glory of thy people Israel,"—that was a suggestive sight, I say, when this Carpenter's Son, so introduced into the world, and so predicted by the prophets, in connection with the Temple, appeared in the Temple, at the age of twelve years, "sitting in the midst of the doctors, both hearing them and asking them questions," so that "all that heard him were astonished at his understanding and answers." And more suggestive was it because of his vindication of his conduct in leaving his father and mother to appear thus in the house of the Lord, in the words, "Wist ye not that I must be about my Father's business?" And, in perfect consistence with this business of his Father's

215

house, which was to be rebuilt and enlarged by him, was the fact that " he went down with them, and came to Nazareth, and was subject unto them," working at the carpenter's bench, with his Father's ideal house before his mind. And in perfect harmony with both facts, " he increased in wisdom and stature, and in favor with God and man." That this ideal House of God, predicted by the prophets, symbolized by the Tabernacle and Temple, was literally before his mind, may be repeated and established, as we turn to the consideration of the Carpenter's Son as he appears in the gospel. Let us consider, as in his mind,

I. *This Temple-Idea.*

1. This idea he would have as a good and thoughtful man. The original concept of the human mind, with regard to God, is associated with the idea of worship. Worship by man implies locality for the worshipper and the worshipped, and here the house or temple idea begins. Hence, Jehovah, referring to Cain's sin, said, "a sin-offering lieth at the door." Jacob called a pile of stones, dedicated to God, " Bethel," the house of God. Every altar erected anywhere, whether in grove or on mountain-top, involved the idea of a house of God. Hence the altars and temples for all gods by all peoples and in all times. This is a universal testimony to this innate conception of the human mind that for the worship of God, there must be a Temple. And the better and the more thoughtful the man the more dis-

tinct would be the idea and desire and effort to give it realization.

2. But, the Carpenter's Son was also a Jew. By divine command, Moses embodied this idea into the Tabernacle, and Solomon into the Temple. This gave the idea a sensible realization—a "local habitation and a name." Henceforth the Jew associated all worship with a visible house of God. This, to the Jew, was the very abode of God. Whether in the ends of the earth or in the depths of the sea, the eyes of the pious Jew were turned toward Jerusalem. The instinctive cry of his heart was, "If I forget thee, O Jerusalem!" And Jerusalem meant "the Temple." Here appears a difference between the pagan mind and the Jewish mind. The pagan had, with regard to his metropolitan city, the political idea most prominent. He built the city, then he erected a temple to his God. The chief thought and concern was Athens, Ephesus, Rome; then the Temple to Minerva, to Diana, to Jupiter. Not so with the Hebrew. Jerusalem was the city of the Temple; and not the Temple a sacred house in Jerusalem. The tribes went up to Jerusalem, wherever they were, because there was the house of God. The fact of the supremacy of the Temple-idea might be illustrated in the psalms, the prophecies, the worship and all the history of this people. But, a striking illustration is found in the rebuilding of the Temple by the decree of Cyrus. The book of Ezra indicates clearly that the longing of the captive Jew, and the order of this eastern monarch, whose mind was influenced by the prophecy of Isaiah

and the wishes of Ezra, had prime reference, not to the rebuilding of Jerusalem, but to the rebuilding of the Temple. The city was merely the necessary surrounding of the Temple. The pagan enemies of the Jews, Sanballat, Tobiah and the rest, who had before them the political idea of a capital city or a king, always refer to the building of the walls and the city; but Ezra and Cyrus speak rather of the building of the Temple. Hence, after the Temple was finished, it is said that "the city was great but the houses were few." Thus the Temple-idea was the main Jewish idea of God's worship. And the mind of the Carpenter's Son was formed in the same Temple-idea mould, and he had awful reverence for his Father's house. With what indignation he drove out the money-changers; and was it not because of the Temple that he made the bitter lament: "O Jerusalem, Jerusalem! . . . Behold, your house is left unto you desolate!"

3. But he, more than man and Jew, had the divine mind, with regard to worship and the Temple. He suggested it when he told the woman of Samaria that neither in Jerusalem nor in Mount Gerizim would be confined the worship of him, who, as a spirit, is to be worshipped in spirit and in truth. The protomartyr Stephen also had the idea of the Master-builder, when he said: "Solomon built him an house. Howbeit the Most High dwelleth not in temples made with hands; as saith the prophet, Heaven is my throne and earth is my footstool: what house will ye build me? saith the Lord: or what is the place of my rest? Hath not my

hand made all these things?" These words raise the mind to the very idea of the temple the Carpenter's Son came to erect for the divine glory, which is to compass earth and heaven and all things made by his hands, and to be infinite and everlasting. This is the original divine Temple-idea; this was the idea fixed as a model before the mind of the Carpenter's Son; this was the idea that his co-workers and the expounders of the doctrine of God's house had before their minds. Max Müller's "Science of Thought" holds that language is the best exponent of mind; and the language of Christ and his apostles clearly indicate this ever-present idea. Notice the expressions of the Master-builder: "Upon this rock will I build my church;" "The keys of the kingdom of heaven;" "Strive to enter the strait gate;" "Ye cannot enter the kingdom;" "In my Father's house are many mansions." Notice the ear-marks on the language of his apostolic co-workers: No sooner did Peter, James and John see him transfigured, with Moses and Elias, than they proposed to erect "three tabernacles." In referring to the progress of the Church, all of them are full of such expressions as "corner-stone," "foundations," "lively stones," "builders," "built up," "framed together," "head of the corner," "earthly house of this tabernacle," "house not made with hands," "edifying," "household of God," "gates," "walls," "New Jerusalem." In our day the church-house is called "the church;" and the end of the ministry, for the believing, is "the edifying of the body of Christ." Excepting the word God, there are perhaps no words used so often in the Bible as words implying building, literal, spiritual and ecclesiastical, which are used no less than three thousand times. This is not strange in a book specifically descriptive of the construction and constructors of the Temple of God. And for the realizing of this great edification, the Master-builder comprehends every part of his religious economies, every object of every department of creation, as well as all providences, plans and purposes: and this Temple may be now more methodically considered under the heads of its Foundations, its Material, its Workers, its Methods, its Gradual Construction, its Prospects of Success and Final Consummation. Having considered the Temple-idea, we shall consider next,

II. *The Temple-Foundations.*

1. The foundation must be deeply, broadly and most substantially laid. (1.) A peculiarity of this temple is that it is to be everlasting. This is involved in the statement, " The gift of God is eternal life." Other gifts of life were not everlasting—neither the life of man nor of angel. But this creation is to have no end. It must be founded, therefore, deeper than the foundations of nature. It must be founded on the being of Jehovah himself. This is implied in its corner-stone, the Divine Lamb, being slain before the foundation of the world. This temple belongs to the original conception of the divine mind, which was to be realized by the creation of all other things. It is identified with the very being of the almighty and eternal. The

foundation is laid in the very essence of God. Hence his purposes, his plans, his providences, all have reference to this construction. Hence, the Father saith to the Son, "Thy throne, O God, is forever and ever." No catastrophe is ever to overthrow this Temple, as the Temple at Jerusalem, the temple of human nature, the temple of angelic nature, was overthrown. This is the ground of the perfect hope of God's servants, and their perfect love which casteth out all fear. "There remaineth, therefore, a rest—a Sabbath-keeping—for the people of God," in that Temple made not with hands, eternal in the heavens. (2.) And how broad must be the foundation? It must be broader than the foundation of nature; for all nature redeemed and holy is to be included within its dimensions: it must be broader than universal convictions; because the innate sense of the creature can never be co-extensive with the moral attributes of the Creator, which are to be represented by this Temple: it must be broader than the expanse of creation or of thought or of conception ever reached by the wing of the loftiest of the intelligences of the universe; for the plan of this Temple and its construction is declared to be a mystery to them. "The measuring rod" is a favorite instrument in prophetic visions of this house; but nothing short of the measuring rod that laid off the divine ideal of that Temple—which was the eternal love of the Father in the Son—could take the measurement of its realization, though Paul prayed with holy ambition that, with all saints, we might "comprehend the breadth and the length, the height and the depth, and to know the love of Christ, which passeth knowledge, being filled with all the fullness of God." As now the mind of man, by aid of the appliances of science, reaches the limits of conceivable distance in the expanse of the physical world, only to find that that apparent limit is the starting point of distance infinitely greater, so in the endless future will there be discoveries of the foundations of this Temple only to lead on to further discoveries, the real limits of which are only short of the limitless building conception of the divine nature. Theoretically and truly, the creature cannot, in any regard, be equal to the Creator, the finite to the infinite; but, so far as the created mind can apprehend, they may be, in the progressive cycles of eternity, one, indivisible and co-everlasting. Is this not involved in the redeemed life being "hid with Christ in God?" (3.) And most substantially laid must be this foundation. The blocks of truth must be more than granite-like in their gravity, their compactness, their disintegratedness, their everlastingness. Some of these truths we have noticed in former economies of God, laid in the foundation, as, for instance, the divine unity, and sacrifice, and election, and presence among men, and retribution, and universal conviction and labors with regard to the realization of his eternally-conceived and purposed and decreed Temple of glory. In the gospel these were all confirmed, and other great blocks of truth superadded. The corner-stone itself was reset, in the actual blood of "the head of the corner," in the awful mysteries of Geth-

semane and Calvary. " Christ before Pilate," so graphically depicted by Munkacsy, but more graphically by
the pencil of inspiration, was fearfully symbolic of that
governmental apprehension and condemnation, whereby
" he that knew no sin was made sin for us that we
might be made the righteousness of God in him," and
to which Peter refers on the day of Pentecost in these
mystic words: " Him, being delivered by the determinate counsel and foreknowledge of God, ye have taken,
and by wicked hands have crucified and slain." Here
was laid a great block, as to vicarious atonement and
justification by faith. The divine incarnation had demonstration in the miracle-working Carpenter's Son,
whose doctrine of the spirituality of the divine Temple
was grandly illustrated in his Sermon on the Mount. In
these facts were involved the divine Trinity and grace,
and human regeneration, redemption, adoption and sanctification. The resurrection and ascension of the Carpenter's Son, and his gift of the Holy Spirit, established
his own eternal priesthood and the bodily resurrection of
those united with him, who here are "a royal priesthood,
a holy nation," and hereafter are to be made "kings and
priests unto God." These blocks of foundation-truth were
laid in the gospel, and made the hope of the believer,
entering into the holy of holiest in the heavenly fane,
"sure and stedfast." These are samples of the "living
rocks" on which the house of God was founded, so that
"the gates of hell shall not prevail against it." It is
upon these, and similar truths, that are based the divine
promises, which are "yea and amen in Christ Jesus."

2. In laying these elements of the foundation of his house, in the mind and heart of his generation, the Carpenter's Son had no little difficulty, as well as his workmen, because of the erroneous and enormous views entertained with regard to the foundation of the typical house of Israel. Hence the denunciations by the Master-builder of the Scribes and Pharisees, who were maliciously blind guides leading the blind; the impressive parabolic teaching of him that spake "as never man spake," accompanied by his practical and persuasive devotion to the people; the powerful arguments for the doctrines of grace made by the apostle to the Romans and Galatiaus, and in other inspired writings of the gospel. The true character of the Jewish economy was fully elucidated in the Epistle to the Hebrews, in which is shown that, in all its ordinances and paraphernalia, it was only "the shadow of things to come." But the gospel was not only "a stumbling-block to the Jew," it was "an offence to the Greek." The pagan mind was appealed to on the ground of its own profoundest convictions and most sacred practices; it being only possible to realize, in the Triune God and his Temple, what they were groping after in their innumerable divinities and their dreams of Utopia and golden ages. To many Jews, led to look from Jerusalem the fallen to "Jerusalem the golden," the Carpenter's Son was revealed as their promised Messiah; and by a greater number of pagans he was accepted as the personal and divine embodiment of all the good elements of their multitudinous gods. Thus, finally, the foundations were established thoroughly, not

merely *de jure* but *de facto*, which are described as "the foundations of the apostles and prophets, Jesus Christ himself being the chief corner-stone."

III. *Temple Material.*

1. This must be holy. The washing services, the selections and the rejections of the Tabernacle and the Temple illustrated this. The clean and the unblemished animal was to be offered; the diseased and the unclean worshipper was excluded; the Gentile was to have no entrance into the court of the Lord. The laver was a prominent feature in the Lord's house. The Tabernacle and every article of it were anointed with oil, for sanctifying. Thus shall nothing defiled by sin have place in the Temple of God. (1.) Before material nature shall be incorporated into the divine kingdom the last remnant of the curse shall be removed. (2.) If angels be unholy, they cannot belong to this house of the Lord. (3.) And what of man? The blood of Christ cleanseth from all sin. The Lord Jesus is made unto the believer wisdom, and righteousness, and sanctification, and redemption. In the righteousness of Christ, imputed by faith, he is holy in the sight of God. Hence it is written: "Ye are washed: ye are clean." As the oil on Aaron's head ran down over his body, so the anointed Christ anoints all his church. Nor is this merely ceremonial. As disbelief is the essence of sin, faith is the essence of holiness. This is the spirit of the believer, who is a new creature in Christ Jesus. Hence it is written: "He cannot sin because the seed

15

of God remaineth in him." This needs be so, for "flesh and blood cannot inherit the kingdom of God." Hence it is also written: "Ye must be born again." The *must* is emphatic, because the natural man "discerneth not the things of God, neither indeed can he, because they are spiritually discerned." Nicodemus could not understand this; but the great soul-builder repeated: "Marvel not that I say unto you, ye must be born again; for except a man be born of water and the Spirit, he cannot see the kingdom of heaven." This regeneration involved all holiness as the acorn involves the oak. The Jews boasted themselves the children of Abraham; but they were rebuked by the family-builder, who declared that from the stones he could raise up children unto Abraham. The dead must be revived, whether Jew or Gentile. This doctrine infuriated the "so-called" children of Abraham. But the Carpenter's Son showed how far they were from the kingdom of heaven, by crying: "Ye generation of vipers, how can ye escape the damnation of hell!" The invariable test to all was, "Ye must be born again." The Apostle Peter describes the material more fully thus: "If so be ye have tasted that the Lord is gracious, to whom coming as unto a living stone, disallowed indeed of men, but chosen of God and precious, ye also, as lively stones, are built up a spiritual house, an holy priesthood to offer up spiritual sacrifices acceptable to God by Jesus Christ . . . Unto you therefore that believe, he is precious; but unto them which be disobedient, the stone which the builders disallowed, the same is made the head of the corner, and a stone of stumbling and a rock of offence even to them which stumble at the word, being disobedient; whereunto also they were appointed. But ye are a chosen generation, a royal priesthood, an holy nation, a peculiar people: that ye should show forth the praises of him who hath called you out of darkness into his marvellous light." And the judicial and personal holiness of man is the key-note of the holiness of all material of this Temple of God.

2. The material is valuable. Solomon erected his symbolic Temple with the most precious and costly material. The worth of the material of the Temple symbolized might be inferred from the inestimable price paid for it—even the blood of the Son of God. Its holiness implies its value, involving the main elements of beauty, strength, durability, harmony, and Godlikeness. In the temple of nature each creature was to reflect something of its Maker; so the temple of grace, in part and in whole, is to show forth the excellence of the God of grace. St. Paul's, in London, is called the monument of its builder, Sir Christopher Wren; so this temple is to celebrate the glory of its architect and maker, God.

3. And abundant is to be the material. The vastness of the foundations implies the vastness of the superstructure. The prophetic city of the Lord was " four square." The height and breadth of this Temple will be equal to its length and depth. Here is room for good material of every kind, from every kingdom and every age of the universe. This was suggested by the

variety and the quantity of material, obtained from far and near, with which Solomon's Temple was built. The expanse of creation is the field for the collecting of matter and spirit for the Lord's house. Indeed, it is to embody the whole of the good and God-honoring of the universe.

4. But the material is all prepared. As the masons shape and adorn each block of marble for the great palace of the king, so there is exactly the work needed on every piece of the selected material to make it fit for its place in the Lord's house. The divine providence is as far reaching as the limits of creation, and, like the long arms of the lofty derrick that extends over and revolves around the foundations of the erecting edifice, picks up the prepared material everywhere, the world over, and sets each piece exactly in its place in the up-building Temple of the Lord.

IV. *Temple Workers.*

In his letter to the Romans, chapter eight and verses twenty-eight and twenty-nine, the Apostle Paul involves in a statement, with regard to the perpetual and universal welfare of God's children, the general principle that what is purposed and predestined in the divine mind will be realized by the co-operation of all that comes from the divine hands. If it is true that all things work together for the believer's predestined conformity to the divine image, it is equally true that all things combine to conform the Temple of God's glory to the ideal eternally formed in the divine mind. This

principle of "all things" working thus is as applicable
to the least creature and circumstance, and relation and
event as to the greatest. The use that the Great Teacher
made of the mote, the gnat, the stone, the seed, the
lily, the vine, the bird of the air, the beast of the field,
as well as the most ordinary affairs and events of human
life, is suggestive and illustrative of this principle.
The ox of Isaiah, and the ass of Balaam give praise to
the Almighty as truly as the choir of the Temple, the
chorus of the angelic host. And not only things seen.
Below the atom and the animalcule is the hidden law,
which the Creative Father hides out of sight, as parents
hide Easter-eggs from their children, that the children
of men may find them and rejoice in what are called
human "inventions;" by which also they are greatly
improved. And how great the building up of the
divine glory by the discovery of the metals of the earth,
the forces of steam and electricity, as well as the laws
of the waves of the sea and the winds of the heavens?
The industrious polyp no more builds the coral reef
than it builds the Temple of God; and "the cricket on
the hearth" chirps his praises as truly as chants the music
of the spheres. Not only "the heavens," but the earth
and the sea and all that in them is, "declare the glory
of God!" This deep laid building-instinct crops out
in the vocabulary of man, in all the arts and sciences to
whose development he applies his mind, and the very
terms prompted by this instinct are suggestive of praise
to the great Master-builder of all. What expressions
are more common than "voice-building;" "health-

building;" "character-building;"   "trade-building;"
"education-building;" "civilization-building;" "na-
tional-building"?   A lower edifice man has before him
in conducting the works implied by these and similar
expressions, but he is doing none the less the highest
and the grandest work, as the mason that worked at the
base of the smallest pillar in St. Peter's, was as truly a
builder on that grandest of human structures as the
erector of the majestic dome said to canopy the tomb of
the great Apostle, on whom the church is said to be
built.   And what Temple-building has been done by
the leaden type, the white-sailed commerce, the civiliza-
tions of man, the history of the nations! Read of the
last in the divine prophecies and providences as fulfilled
in human events; the Temple-building of the others is
seen and read now of all men.   Nor is there any evil
in the universe that is not working in the same direction—widespread suffering on earth; endless torments
in hell! Lucifer builds as well as Gabriel the Lord's
house; as Sanballat and Tobiah did, though Ezra and
Nehemiah did not know it.   The principle, in universal
application, is fully established in the divine declaration: "All things are yours, and ye are Christ's and
Christ is God's."

But it is with a small part of this building-force that
"the Carpenter's Son in the Gospel" has specially to do—
with the temple-builder man, regenerate and consecrated
to the work for which he came into being.   Though
relatively small in number, yet this is one of the most
important builders, and really not a few in number.

The part of the human family, predestined to do this work consciously and willingly, were to be gathered from every class, every age and every clime. There was need for talents of every kind and every degree, and the constant employment of every gift. The powers of man, mental, moral, spiritual as well as physical, are only instruments which the Master has given for the carrying forward of this structure in all its varied and endless departments, as many as the occupations and duties and possibilities of worthy life. In this corps and for certain works on the Temple, the Carpenter's Son does not employ forced labor, as he does in insensate and diabolic nature. But, as the builders of the Tabernacle brought their offerings voluntarily, joyfully, abundantly, so must be the gifts and labors of the spiritually elect—the household of the Carpenter's Son. Hence, as has been said, their spirit must be regenerate, faithful and loving —ready to do and to suffer their Lord's will. Heavy burdens are to be borne in the erection of God's house— many self-denials, many pangs, many deaths. One of the greatest builders said: "I die daily." The chief builder laid the foundations in his blood! This suggests that a peculiarity of these builders is that they are also a part of the material of the edifice. This is an inspiring thought, that not only is it true that self-building is temple-building, but temple-building is self-building. Laboring for the conformity of God's house is the means for the laborers' predestined conformity to the image of the Son of God! Wicked men build God's house and are cast away, as the nations corrected Israel, and were then broken themselves; but the very effort to do God's will is the sanctifying and glorifying process with regard to the personal temple of the Lord. This building-work, therefore, should be ever before the mind, as the ideal is before the sculptor, the model before the builder. As the mason works on the block of marble to shape and adorn it, so should the temple-builder work; and work should be—if the figure may be continued—with the white apron of honest service, with the square and plummet of divine truth, with the compasses of faith stretched out after the circuit of the vast edifice to be erected; and, above all, he must work with a heart of love, looking above the work to the Master-builder, who says to every true-hearted workman, "I will guide thee with mine eye." And as he works he must study, prayerfully study, the autobiographies of the Master-builder in the volumes of nature and providence and revelation; and all his thoughts and knowledge thus acquired he should consecrate to the energizing and directing of the constructive principle of his nature, with reference to this God-ordained edification, personal, social, ecclesiastical, spiritual, universal, everlasting, divine!

And let these conscious and conscientious workers on the Lord's house be cheered with the fact of the universal co-operation that they have in this edification. The universe is God's workshop, preparing and adjusting material for the temple of his final glory. The thought of non-success is a crime in the believer's heart. Let the builder realize that he and God's people are a part of the structure, and the certainty of their personal success and final triumph is the certainty of the success and triumph of the Lord's Temple. Let the underlying principle of these words following be applied to the edifying house of God : "If God be for us, who can be against us? He that spared not his own Son, but delivered him up for us all, how shall he not with him freely give us all things? . . . Nay in all these things we shall be more than conquerors through him that loved us. For I am persuaded that neither death, nor life, nor angels, nor principalities, nor powers, nor things present, nor things to come, nor height, nor depth, nor any other creature shall be able to separate us from the love of God, which is in Christ Jesus our Lord."

V. *Temple Methods.*

As to the methods for executing this work, they are as varied as the material selected, the workers employed, the circumstances surrounding, the forces engaged, and the laws of the world, material, mental, moral and spiritual: as varied and many as the thoughts, the purposes, the providences, and the resources of Jehovah. But in the Gospel, the Carpenter's Son confines his methods to such as are appropriate for what may be called church-building work. That is the distinctive mission of the Gospel, and the methods prescribed are clearly indicated. For this church-building there are several requisites :

1. *Perfect Pattern.*—This was strikingly set forth in the erection of the Tabernacle. A strange emphasis is

given to this by the fact that Moses repeats to the people the exact directions given by the Lord in the mount; and when he builds he reiterates the same particulars as having been realized. Thus in the edification of the churches, by the introduction of new material and the establishment of the old, there must be a constant reference to the law and the testimony of the gospel. For everything there should be, "Thus saith the Lord."

2. *Plain Preaching.*—By preaching is meant the proclamation of the Gospel. The command is: "Preach the word." There is room for illustration from every direction—from the nest-building sparrow, the mound and palace-building man and the tower-erecting angel; but all illustration must only make more plain the gospel, which is the wisdom of God and the power of God. This seems a simple method, but God's greatest achievements are by the simplest means, whereby the true power is discovered. It is by this method, obviously insufficient in itself, that the Master-builder has the opportunity of evincing, by his Spirit, the omnipotence of his hand. God is jealous of his glory.

3. *Patient Prayer.*—Powerful were the enemies to the erection of the Lord's house in the days of Ezra and Nehemiah. But more powerful are they in the days of the Gospel. We contend with the powers of darkness—the prince of the power of the air: the god of this world! Most rational, then, is the declaration: "Not by might, nor power, but by my Spirit, saith the Lord." Hence the divine command: "Pray without ceasing." And it is because of this necessity that "prayer is the

Christian's vital breath." Many may be the obstructions to the immediate answer to prayer; but, made according to the divine promise, it shall be inevitably answered. In some fifteen lines, in the seventh chapter of Matthew, the Carpenter's Son declares seven times, in one form or another, that there shall be reply to the seeking and knocking of patient prayer. The adversary of souls may seem to prevail, but the emphatic promise encourages the praying soul: "Shall not God avenge his own elect which cry day and night unto him?"

4. *Plenteous Pay.*—The light of the gospel is free; but the candle-stick is very expensive. This is designedly so, that faith and love may be tested by the free gifts of money which represents all values among men. The vast expenditures on the Tabernacle and Temple were nothing in comparison with the riches required to be lavished on this greater house of the Lord. Hence the enormous wealth given to God's people under the gospel. In our own country the wealth of the Lord's professed workmen is estimated at eleven billions of dollars; and the net annual increase of their wealth four hundred and fifty millions of dollars. And with lavish hand these riches are employed in the building of the Lord's house. In addition to what is expended for the general civilization, which is the scaffold about the house of the Lord, the sum of eighty millions of dollars is spent yearly in the United States for purposes of religion. But ten times that amount might be profitably spent in this service, which should most engross the heart of the lover of Christ's kingdom. In the apoc-

ryphal book of Esdras it is related that the wise young
man to whom Darius promised to give whatever he
might ask, asked that the king would fulfil his vow to
rebuild the Lord's house. Before the heroic Judith goes
forth to bring back the head of Holofernes, the general
of the besieging Assyrians, she casts herself before God
and implores: "Throw down their strength in thy
power, and bring down their force in thy wrath: for
they have purposed to defile thy sanctuary, and to
pollute the tabernacle where thy name resteth, and to
cast down with the sword the horn of thy altar." What
lessons of absorbing love to God's house the Jew ever
gives to the Christian!

5. *Perpetual Progression.* — The Carpenter's Son
ordered that "beginning *from* Jerusalem," his fellow-
laborers should establish the truth in "all nations."
The field for church-extension is the world. The human race is to be reclaimed; and the name of the
Master-builder made great "unto the ends of the earth."
The church-building idea is that of constant expansion.
For this prayer should be ever made, and money should
be ever given, and preachers should be in increasing numbers ever employed. The heart's deepest and most per-
sistent supplication should be: "Thy kingdom come;
thy will be done in earth as it is in heaven." Lavish
has been the expenditure on the Lord's house; but it
has been that part of the house which is nearest *home.*
The ratio of the offerings of the Lord's house at home
and the Lord's house abroad is the ratio of 400 to 1; and
the ratio of ministerial labor is as 500 to 1; and of all

Christian labor as 650 to 1. Alas for this exhibit, in view of these facts:

1st. That there is perhaps no man or woman in the United States who has not heard of Christ, while the number in pagan lands is so great that if they should file before us, one in five seconds, it would take more than a hundred years to count them!

2d. That the last command of our ascending Lord was to disciple the nations, on obedience to which is based the promise: "And, lo, I am with you alway, even unto the end of the world."

3d. That the true ground for seeking the divine blessing is that it may be expended on others, the reflex influence of which brings yet further blessing upon our own selves. This is illustrated in the Psalmist's prayer: "God be merciful unto us, and bless us, and cause his face to shine upon us, *that thy way may be known upon earth*, thy saving health among ALL NATIONS . . . Then shall the earth yield her increase: and God, even our own God, shall bless us."

These facts should broaden our views of church-building, at least until our ideas and hopes and labors shall be co-extensive with the divine decree: "Ask of me and I shall give thee the heathen for an inheritance and the uttermost parts of the earth for thy possession." The joyous toil of the co-worker with the Carpenter's Son should be to aid the realization of that broad edification of the church when the acclaim shall ascend from earth to heaven, "The kingdoms of this world are become the kingdom of the Lord and of his Christ."

And this is only a stepping-stone for the infinitely wider temple-work of the Lord, compassing the highest intelligences of the wide-spread universe. Hear what Paul says: "Unto me . . . is this grace given that I should preach among the gentiles the unsearchable riches of Christ: and to make all men see what is the fellowship of the mystery which from the beginning of the world hath been hid in God, who created all things by Jesus Christ; *to the intent that now unto the princi-palities and powers in heavenly places might be known by the church the manifold wisdom of God, according to the eternal purpose which he purposed in Christ Jesus our Lord* . . . of whom the whole family in heaven and earth is named."

GRADUAL CONSTRUCTION AND FINAL CONSUMMA-TION OF TEMPLE.

I. *Gradual Construction.*

To represent this fully would require a picture of the progress of the universe for nineteen hundred years. All that shall be attempted is to give several indications of the progressive construction of a small part of the sacred edifice which pertains specially to our race and world.

1. Nineteen hundred years ago, there were one hundred and twenty names of the Lord's house, unknown and despised; now there are great nations bearing the name and exerting the most powerful influence over the earthly interests and destiny of the human family.

2. Nineteen hundred years ago the name of the Carpenter's Son was known in a little strip of country in dimensions not more than one hundred miles by one hundred and sixty; now there is not a country or province or state on our round globe where this name is not known and worshipped.

3. During these nineteen centuries there have been many variations in the rate of the work's progress, yet the work has ever gone on, as indicated by the growing number of workmen.

(1) In the first century there were 500,000 professed workers for the Carpenter's Son; in the second, 2,000,-000; in the third, 5,000,000; in the fourth, 10,000,-000; in the fifth, 15,000,000; in the sixth, 20,000,000; in the seventh, 24,000,000; in the eighth, 30,000,000; in the ninth, 50,000,000; in the tenth, 70,000,000; in the eleventh, 80,000,000; in the twelfth, 75,000,000; in the thirteenth, 80,000,000; in the fourteenth, 100,-000,000; in the fifteenth, 125,000,000; in the sixteenth, 155,000,000; in the eighteenth, 200,000,000; and, judging from the ratio of increase in the former part of the nineteenth century, at the close of it there will be over 300,000,000 professed workers for Jesus. These figures aggregate the present population of the world. Suppose every man and woman and child of the fourteen hundred millions on earth were professed laborers for the Carpenter's Son, we would have some conception of the progress of this great temple on earth !

(2) And during these nineteen hundred years, under the shadow of the uprising house of the Lord, (a) How

great has been the progress of the thought, the literature, the art, the science, the commerce, the manufactures, the agriculture, the jurisprudence, the civil liberty, the good will, the benevolence, the goodness, the godliness among men. (b) These, and countless other benefits, are the outcome of the Lord's house, and in turn furnish aid and material for its edification. (c) But, the greatest progress is to be seen in the unseen history of these billion and a half of loving and faithful builders during these nineteen centuries. How many secret battles did they fight with sin and Satan? How many victories did they win in the name of the Lord? How many their self-sacrifices, their good deeds, their sufferings, their martyrdoms for the Lord? How much interest they occasioned among rejoicing angels in heaven and guardian spirits on earth? What miracles of grace were performed by the Carpenter's Son on their behalf? What the frequent disappointments and consternation in the kingdom of darkness at the progress of this house of the Lord? As far as the wide-spread universe is, the work of this temple-building has been going on during these nineteen centuries.

(3) And what is the present outlook? (a) In the last ten years, the increase of laborers among pagan nations has been three and a half per cent. greater than in our own civilized land. (b) The cross is displayed in two hundred and twenty-four languages of the human family, and in one hundred and forty-eight millions of Bibles in circulation. (c) In the past fifty years, two millions of souls have been gathered in "as workers

together with God," called also "God's building."
Bishop Simpson says: The world is full of promise.
Everything looks cheerful. Never have there been so
many Bibles, so many schools, so many sermons, so
many workers for God, since the light first dawned on
the garden of Eden. (d) But the influence of the Carpenter's Son, unlike the distinguished of the earth,
growing stronger and stronger as the ages go on, cannot
be calculated by statistics. His cross has permeated the
literature and modified or overthrown the governments
of men not conducive to his work; his natal days, in
the flesh and in the spirit, are celebrated by the civilized
world. And this influence is disintegrating the institutions of sin, and gathering up vast and valuable material
for the establishment of grace. His providence is
subordinating all art and science to this end; and, in
fact, it is apparent that the world's civilization is only
"a scaffold for the erection of the Lord's house." All
creation, visible and invisible, unites with the persons
of the Godhead covenanted for this purpose, to carry
forward over every obstacle, natural and supernatural,
human and diabolic, to its perfect and glorious completion, the Lord's house erecting by the Carpenter's Son.

II. *Final Consummation.*

1. The certainty of this glorious consummation rests
upon these sure foundations:

(1) The eternal conception and ideal of this temple of
glory of the divine mind, in relation to which were his
purposes and plans and predestinations, for the execu-
16

tion of which the eternal council of the Godhead was formed and the whole universe was created and has been preserved and controlled.

(2) The mediatorial glory of the Carpenter's Son is involved in this consummation, the failure of which would make his varied manifestations, and revelations, and symbols, and his incarnation and sacrifice and resurrection, and commission, and ascension, and intercession, and gift of the Spirit, and promises to his workmen, all in vain, and would indeed virtually overthrow the divine throne itself!

(3) The word and the oath of the Father have been given to the Son. This is the accomplishment of the work; for God is truth, and with him there is no time. In the divine being the Temple is already complete. Time drags on with the creature, and he looks to the future with hope; but with the Carpenter's Son there is already the celebration of the eternal glory.

2. And what is to be the sum of this great consummation?

(1) The race of man, broken into diverse and conflicting nations, is to be reunited in common faith and love as the redeemed part of the family of God.

(2) Physical nature, groaning and travailing because of moral evil, shall be restored to the perfection of which its Creator said : "It is good;" hence "the earnest expectation of the creature waiteth for the manifestation of the sons of God."

(3) Heaven and earth shall be restored in relations intimate and fraternal. Paul speaks of the Lord's

family being in heaven and earth : and declares that in the dispensation of the fulness of times all things in heaven and earth shall be gathered together in one— even in Christ.

(4) The whole universe, material and immaterial, known and unknown, shall be united in one stupendous, magnificent whole, which the Greeks called τὸ πᾶν, described by Humboldt as essential unity with infinite diversity, but which is the realization of the divine ideal of a universal and everlasting Temple, whose shekinah is God himself, whose worship is the homage of the universe, and whose arch dome shall reverberate ever with acclaims to its architect and builder, who was once the crucified, but is now the glorified, Carpenter's Son.

CHAPTER XXIV.

IN GLORY.

The Son of man standing on the right hand of God.—Acts vii. 56.

THAT was a signal occasion when the Carpenter's Son led his disciples out as far as Bethany, and having given them instructions and blessed them, ascended into a cloud and disappeared from their sight; but, they transfixed in gaze, stood looking up into the heavens, doubtless following in imagination the vision of his ascension, until they were brought to themselves by the appearance of angels, saying: "The same Jesus that is taken up from you into heaven shall so come as ye have seen him go into heaven."

This ascension was natural and necessary. He went back to the Father, having done the work the Father gave him to do, because he came out from the Father. Of his relation with the other world, the reader of his earthly career is kept constantly reminded. He appeared once—in the hour of transfiguration—in heavenly glory. Angels declared his conception by the Holy Ghost and his name "God with us," shouted hosannahs at his birth, ministered unto him in temptation and agonies, and received him into glory. Evil spirits knew him, and even fell down and worshipped him. He communed constantly with the Father, prayed unto him, and agonized in his holy presence, and died commending

244

his spirit to the keeping of him whose voice had come to him from heaven more than once, saying, "This is my beloved Son." He had prayed, in the presence of his disciples, "And now, O Father, glorify thou me with thine own self with the glory which I had with thee before the world was." And glimpses of this glorified state are given in the Word. The heavens were opened to Stephen, and he saw the Carpenter's Son standing on the right hand of God. On the isle of Patmos, John saw him with awfully glorious appearance surrounded by the praising hosts of heaven.

But when he ascends to the glory of his Father, does the Carpenter's Son give up his great constructive work? Before his ascension, having before his mind his royal carpentry, he distinctly stated, "In my Father's house are many mansions; if it were not so I should have told you. I go to prepare a place for you, that where I am ye may be also." This idea and promise his disciples kept before them: and when Paul refers to the departure of the saint he words it thus: "If the earthly house of this tabernacle be dissolved, we have a building of God, a house not made with hands, eternal in the heavens."

1. What that house is that the Carpenter's Son is gone to prepare for his people we do not know exactly; nor how long it will be in course of preparation. Being a place, the body of the saint is implied as an inhabitant of it, and the general resurrection may not come until the full preparation, though he said to the thief on the cross, "This day shalt thou be with me in paradise."

The earth was preparing a long time for man : the kingdom of heaven among men, a long time for the coming of the Carpenter's Son : and many may be the years and ages before the heavenly mansions shall be complete.

2. But, meanwhile, how is the glorified Carpenter's Son employed? Is his mind and hand less engrossed in his mediatorial work than when on earth?

(1) His first recorded act in glory was the fulfilment of his promise to send the Holy Spirit to reprove the world of sin and righteousness and judgment to come, which he did in that marvellous Pentecostal outpouring in which his presence was indicated by fire and by which multitudes from all parts of the world were brought to the feet of the despised Carpenter's Son. And all the grace received, and all the power manifested, and all the success obtained by his disciples, in preaching the word, in planting churches, in working miracles, in saving souls, in escaping dangers, in enduring persecutions, in writing epistles, whether in Palestine, Asia Minor or Europe, were freely avowed to have come from him. Thus has it been in all the ages since, the world over, even unto the present day. The testimony of every believing soul is: "Not unto us, O Lord, not unto us, but unto thy name, give glory!" So preserved is the intimate and vital and conscious relation between him and his people, that his glorified state is sometimes declared to be the state of saints on earth, as when Paul blesses God that his people are blessed "with all spiritual blessings in heavenly places in Christ."

(2) The interests of his people he makes identical with his own. When he smites down the persecuting Saul he asks, Why persecutest thou *me?* In the last day he shall say, " Inasmuch as ye have done it unto one of the least of these my brethren, ye have done it unto me."

(3) But, the revelation is plain that the work he began on earth, he is perfecting in heaven. In the heavenly Tabernacle, of which the tabernacle of earth was only a shadow, he, as a royal High Priest after the order of Melchizedek, is offering the sacrifice of the Lamb of God, slain from the foundation of the world, and making endless intercessions for his people, whereby their consciences are purged from guilt; and whereby the varied duties, personal, social, ecclesiastic, prefigured in the Mosaic ritual and enforced under the gospel economy, may be faithfully performed; the work begun in them brought to completion; and their perseverance to the end made sure.

3. Nor is he unmindful of any interest of his people. In the apocalypse we see him :

(1) Walking among the churches, giving counsel, rebuking, encouraging, in fulfilment of his promise: " Where two or three are gathered together in my name there am I in the midst of them."

(2) He is also the mover of all the history and all the mysteries of grace. It is " the Lamb"—the Carpenter's Son—who is represented as breaking the seven seals, which none other can break.

(3) He has an eye ever to the enemies of his people—

the beast and the dragon and the scarlet harlot. And it is from his hands that come the vials of wrath.

(4) And all the grand representations of the "Revelation," are they not the pictures of the administration of the Carpenter's Son, during the ages, in the interest of the great work of his hands?

4. And the promise of the angels and of his own lips, with regard to his return for the final adjustment of the material of this world, shall be fulfilled in the midst of the glory of the angelic hosts, the sounding of trumpets which shall awake to life the dead bodies of all ages, and with a personal effulgence of glory before which the sun shall pale and the wicked nations of men and the infernal hosts of darkness shall tremble and seek to flee away ; but in which the righteous shall rejoice with joy unspeakable and full of glory. How vast the accession thus to be made to the perfected material and to the glorified worshippers of the eternal Temple of the Lord !

5. But, this does not exhaust the resources of the Carpenter's Son, in the construction of this Temple of the divine praise. His administration over our race is momentous, but his government and work reach much further. Perfect before him is his ideal and predestined temple, which is in course of erection; and his all-seeing eye sweeps over the field of creation, and his all-reaching hand takes hold on material here and there and everywhere, and his wisdom and his power are ever engaged in realizing the end for which all things were made. A human architect and builder, infinitely magnified in

ability and work, would give some idea of the engagement of the Carpenter's Son—supposing that master-builder and architect to be engaged in realizing some grand, life-long ideal of his mind. All that has been said of the heavenly pursuits of the glorified Carpenter's Son, and all that he really does, has reference to this all-comprehending and eternal work. The following words just fall under the eye, in studying the Sunday-school lesson of July 29th, 1888, on "The Tabernacle," which is in harmony with our figure:

"The modern architect, like the one on Sinai, sees the building he is going to construct before the timber has been cut or the ground broken. Gerard von Rile, six hundred years ago, saw the cathedral which has just been completed beside the Rhine at Cologne. Slowly, since the year 1200, German artisans have been copying into stone von Rile's thought, working from his plan, and the cathedral is perfect to-day because it was perfect then. All that God does is in pursuance of a plan, an eternal idea come to utterance."

But how can we take in the glory of that final restitution of all things material and immaterial, human and angelic and divine, and the restored universe as the Temple of God, compassing all good and full of all praises to the Lamb, world without end? God is merciful to our weakness. As he brings down to human comprehension his own infinite and everlasting being in the person of the Carpenter's Son, so he brings down to our capacity his infinite and everlasting house erecting to his glory, in its final completeness, in the glorious picture of the New Jerusalem, with its gates of pearls, its foundations of precious stones, its streets of gold, the river of life proceeding from the throne of the Lamb, who is the light and glory and worship of the place, and upon whose vesture and thigh a name is written— "King of Kings and Lord of Lords."

And this is enough,—this Jerusalem the golden,—for it serves as a back-ground for the sight of Him whom above all the believer wishes to see "face to face."   In Saint Peter's of Rome, only a part of its greatness can be taken in at a time, and many days are needed to study and appreciate its vastness and beauty.   So the cycles of eternity must roll around before the mind can grasp all the glory of the perfected Temple of God. But, as the shekinah was the glory of the Tabernacle and the Temple, and the presence of the "Holy One of Israel" is the glory of the churches of our day, so the glorified Carpenter's Son is the glory of the Lord's Temple, world without end, and we shall "see him as he is."   That sufficeth ; that will suffice for evermore. And even now may we not have a glimpse of him, through the Apocalyptic vision of John?   We have seen "Christ on Calvary."   Here is a sketch of "Christ before Pilate :"

"He stands before Pilate, his hands firmly bound in front of him, his face, though calm and strong, bearing the marks of hunger and sleeplessness and the terrible mental agony through which he has lately passed.   As another has said in describing this picture, 'Though knowing he is to be sentenced to death, there is nothing of hopelessness in his face. He is courageous, though submissive to the will of the Father; not shrinking before the fierce looks and fiercer cries of the angry mob eager for his life, but with calm forbearance and quiet dignity enduring the insults and bitter taunts as one rendered superior to them by the consciousness of his divine mission.' No tremor passes over this wonderful face, no thought of self is betrayed by a single line or movement. He stands erect, though bound, looking into the face of Pilate in a searching way that has caused many to remark that it is Christ who is the real judge and Pilate who is being weighed in the balance."

How different the Carpenter's Son in glory! See the holy picture, not by the Genius-inspired Munkacsy, but by the God-inspired John: "I looked, and, behold, a door was opened in heaven . . . and, behold, a throne, and there was a rainbow round about the throne . . . And round about the throne I saw four and twenty elders sitting, clothed in white raiment; and they had on their heads crowns of gold . . . The four and twenty elders fall down before him that sat on the throne, and worship him that liveth for ever and ever, and cast their crowns before the throne, saying, Thou art worthy, O Lord, to receive glory, and honor, and power: for thou hast created all things, and for thy pleasure they are and were created . . . And they sung a new song, saying, Thou art worthy . . . for thou wast slain, and hast redeemed us to God by thy blood out of every kindred, and tongue, and people, and nation; and hast made us unto our God kings and priests . . . And I heard the voice of

many angels round about the throne . . . and the number
of them was ten thousand times ten thousand, and thousands of thousands; saying with a loud voice, Worthy
is the Lamb that was slain; . . . and every creature which
is in heaven, and on the earth, and under the earth, and
such as are in the sea, and all that are in them, heard
I saying, Blessing, and honor, and glory, and power, be
unto him that sitteth upon the throne, and unto the
Lamb, for ever and ever."

THE END.